# THE RAVEN C

By: Michael F. Spratt

# Preface

What *The Raven Conspiracy* is: A novel showcasing the unconventional characters that are drawn to living in a small beach town on the periphery of the USA. A story that includes many mysteries and a few crimes woven around a casual fun setting.

The characters detailed are derived in part from individuals I have met. Five decades of university teaching and international business can expose you to a lot of the uniqueness in humanity.

A story about people and a location on the fringe of society needs a time period that is equal to the task. The first week of March 2020 was a moment on the brink of awareness. I realized this when I ask the manager of a very successful restaurant on A1A what he thought about the virus being reported in the news. His response, "I haven't heard of it, but it will not affect us. We keep a very clean kitchen."

## 2020 should be a great year

March at Crescent Beach can be magic or maddening or both. The third day of this March started out warm, sunny, and fabulous. Gidget set up her ice cream cart early in the morning.

"Hey lady! Have you got a permit for that thing?" Most people would be a little concerned if they heard the deputy sheriff yelling at them, but this street vendor knew she had nothing to be worried about.

When JP walked up followed by his two large dogs, Gidget coyly said, "I'm so sorry sheriff, are you going to cuff me?" She was halfway serious about flirting with JP but she knew it wouldn't matter. One would think a guy in his mid-50s would be interested in a pretty and fit woman in her early-30s, even if she did have a teenage daughter. Oh well. She would settle for being friends.

Short, petite, and looking cute as ever in a pink crop top and white shorts accented by yellow flip flops, Gidget was ready for her role this spring on the Florida coast. Her ice cream cart was old but well maintained and decorated in pastel colors; the normal heavy customer traffic was mainly powered by the owner's kinetic personality. Ice cream is even better when it's fun to buy.

The standard "uniform" that patrolled this beach was totally atypical of law enforcement in most areas: Hawaiian shirt, khaki cargo shorts and tan cowboy boots with a red lizard stitched in the toe. JP was not trained for policing, but luckily nothing much was needed in that department in this tiny coastal village.

The deputy sheriff asked, "Aren't you getting started a little early this year Gidget? It's only March 3rd, you know. "

"The weather is so fantastic, I just decided to get started. I think this is going to be a wonderful year, and lots of great things are going to happen. I can't wait for the season to start. Hey, I woke up this morning and thought to myself, 'this is a year where the beginning and the end are the same.' Did you ever think of that?"

"What?" The deputy had to admit to himself it was not always easy to understand what this woman was saying, but he always loved the way she said it.

Gidget outlined her great discovery: "It's 2020, get it? Just think the last time it was like this it was 1919 then I guess 1818 and then 1717. It's just crazy, don't you think? "

JP smiled. "Yeah, I get it - that is kind of interesting".

Just as he was about to ask a question, Songbird Wilson zoomed by on a very long skateboard holding a very small yellow surfboard wearing an even smaller yellow bikini.
The expert freestyle surfer yelled, "Hey Mom! Hey JP! Fabulous day."

Gidget called out, "Where are you going?"
The surfer yelled back "Hawaii" as she disappeared around the sidewalk bend that led to the ocean.
Songbird Wilson came from a long line of surfing women; her grandmother surfed, her mother, who had been named after a famous surfer in a movie, also surfed when not selling ice cream. But Songbird was

exceptional, the most famous freestyler on the east coast.

The deputy sheriff tried to put on a serious demeanor. "Ms. Wilson, you know that today is a school day, don't you? Were you aware that your daughter is skipping school so she can go surfing?"

Gidget was super happy to answer, in her own way, "You know the ValCom contest is next month in Miami. Do you think she can win?" After asking the question she knows needs no response, she started pulling sunglasses, flipflops, and little bottles of sunscreen from a bag behind the cart. The ice cream lady started to set them up in a very orderly fashion at the front edge of her cart where she added a little sign that simply said "five dollars."

"JP, all the stuff you got me last summer is selling out. How can I get more?"

The deputy thought about that for a minute; but mainly he thought how it was best for Songbird to surf; she had no real future in school. However, on the waves, she was unbelievable. He knew the younger Ms. Wilson could win any freestyle surf event she entered. Songbird might be the best anywhere. JP was proud to know her.

But how should JP handle the merchandise inquiry at hand? Slowly rubbing the end of his goatee, he said, "Gidget, let me tell you a little secret. I bought all that stuff at the dollar store in Saint Augustine, so I can just go get you some more when you need me to."

Shocked, the vendor replied, "Oh, you're kidding! You paid a dollar for this stuff and I am selling it for five! I feel really bad. How can I ever find the people and give them some of their money back? What should I do? This is awful!"

JP needed to calm her down. "Gidget, you are providing a valuable service - you're providing temporal and location utility."

"I am?" Although she didn't know exactly what the deputy just said, and what it could possibly mean.

"You are an integral part of the economy, and the prices that you have charged are extremely fair!" reassures JP.

"Really?" Now this hard-working lighthearted mom was really confused. How could buying for a dollar and selling for five be fair??

The deputy saw he needed to provide a detailed explanation. "Think of it this way: when someone comes up to buy an ice cream from you and they remember they need sunscreen or they need sunglasses or they need flip-flops instead of street shoes to go to the beach, if they have to get in their car and drive to Saint Augustine it's going to cost them more than four dollars and it will waste their day. YOU are saving them time and money and making their life happier! Just think about that!"

And just as Gidget was trying to think about what JP said, she looked up and saw three early-20s type beach goers followed by two women carrying babies running down the sidewalk, and they were all screaming **"shark shark shark"** – Gidget takes off running for the beach & Songbird in a flash!

# 1

## FBI comes to the Beach

Ricky West spent every penny he inherited in 1965 to build his surf board shop in Crescent Beach. Just east of A1A, the standard 30 foot by 70 foot cinderblock building was nothing fancy, except for the door which Ricky had custom-made to look exactly like a longboard. He did pretty well selling wooden handmade surfboards until fiberglass overtook him in the late 60s.

By 1975 Ricky was so far back on his obligations that the county took the building for the back taxes and it sat empty for twenty-five years. Then somebody at the county decided they had to sell the building or use it, the Sheriff's office volunteered to take it and set it up as an Annex in Crescent Beach.

Mary Carson, a young administrative assistant in Saint Augustine Saint John's County Sheriff's office was picked to head up converting the building to use for law enforcement. She would end up changing her position and becoming the only employee at the Annex from 2002 till 2017. Mary ran the place and kept it looking nice. If there were any reports of crime, which there really were not, it was her job to report them to the Sheriff, which she really never needed to do. Mrs. Carson liked living close to her work and she loved being a part of day-to-day life in Crescent Beach.

In early March 2020, when three FBI agents parked at the Annex, it looked nothing like they had expected it to. Painted light blue with pale yellow trim around the roof, it looked like it belonged in maybe Miami. Palm trees planted all around the front surrounded three parking spaces, which had no cars in them. On the west side of the building a giant planting box ran from the front to the rear end and was filled with blueberry plants. And on the east side another matching giant planting box was filled with milkweed and assorted flowers, which would draw hordes of butterflies in the spring and summer.

As the agents walked in, the reception room looked much more like a cozy living room than a police station. Mary stood up and said in a lively way, "Hi, you're the FBI people. I know you're here to see JP, but would you like a cup of coffee first?"

An extremely tall black agent who was clearly in charge said, "No thank you ma'am."

Mary quickly interjected, "How about tea or soda? I've got some pastries."

The lead agent responded, "We would like to see Deputy Barnett now."

Slightly disappointed, Mary pointed down the hall and said, "It's the only office on the left. If you hit the bathrooms, you've gone too far."

The corridor was short, but it was wide and airy. On the left there were potted plants every three feet, and on the right was a nice picture window that overlooked the butterfly garden. The agents really didn't appreciate all the hard work Mary had put in to making the Annex feel welcoming. When they reached the first door on the left, they saw immediately a large black dog laying on the floor in the corner and then after two steps into the doorway they noticed a large white dog laying in the opposing corner.

JP was sitting at his desk in his typical Hawaiian shirt and cargo shorts with his cowboy boots propped up on the top of the desk. "Hey guys, welcome to Crescent Beach."

Taken aback by the casual atmosphere, there was a moment of silence as the lead agent tried to take in the nature of the office. A framed newspaper article from *Le Monde*, a college diploma, and a cork board full of what looked to be concert tickets hung on the walls behind the desk. No local maps, no chalkboard, nothing displayed to suggest they were in the deputy sheriff's office.

The lead Fed responded, "I'm special Agent Williams, and this is Agent Gonzalez and Agent Sato." He stuck out his hand to shake the local lawman's hand.

The deputy couldn't help but smile as he thought, *This looks just like the Fed: a black guy probably hired in the 80s, a Latino guy probably hired two decades later, and an Asian chick that looks like she just got out of high school. Affirmative action at work!*

"Deputy Barnett, do you find this funny?" ask Williams.

"Sorry, I have a tendency to smile at inappropriate times. I don't know how I got that bad habit, but most people don't seem to mind it. By the way, could we go by first names? All this 'agent this' and 'deputy that' stuff seems a bit much."

"We prefer to keep things professional," said Williams, clearly the dominant agent.

"I understand and I don't want to get off on the wrong foot, but we have a very casual culture here. You guys seem very professional, you're all in black suits, you've all got white shirts, two out of three if you have black ties and you've all got uncomfortable looking shoes. I think things would move more smoothly if we could be a bit more casual."

The deputy looked twice left to right and said, "Ladies first," then stepped forward and held his hand out in front of Agent Sato: "Hi, am Jean Paul Barnett. Everyone calls me JP, and you are?"

The junior agent looked to her team leader for guidance. Williams nodded. "Nice to meet you, JP, I am Agent Betty Sato, you can call me Betty," and shook the deputy's hand.

The Latino agent grabbed JP's hand firmly and looked at him directly. He smiled and said, "George."

The lead agent said, "Martin J.  Williams. If we're playing casual, 'Martin' works fine. Now let's get down to business. Sheriff Richardson told me when I called him this morning that I could work with you and your team on this case. And we have a lead on the unsub for these three terrorist attacks that your community has had."

JP said, "You guys actually say 'unsub'? I thought that was just on TV. And I don't really think this is a terrorist. But whatever you want to call it."

"What do you call it when you have a person of interest that appears to have shot up your beach, poisoned several people, and in a third incident blown up a boat in the intercoastal waterway?" asked Martin.

"Well, I tend to call it a freaking asshole from hell who's got some kind of mental problem that I don't care to figure out. But 'terrorist' I think is overreach for 'this person of interest' (with added air quotes). Can we just her The Bitch?"

Belaying her slight stature, the female agent interjects, "I would prefer you not use the term 'bitch' [as she added her own air quotes]. "It would be good if we move forward towards our objectives. We have two credible sources that indicate that we may be able to close this matter quickly."

Martin quickly added," We are here to invite you to help us interview a woman that we believe goes by the alias J. McCormick. We know she lives in this area, but we cannot seem to find an address."

JP stared up and slowly stroked his goatee.

Williams added, "She may be living on a boat or near the intercoastal somehow, if that helps any."

"JJ Cormack?! Sorry, you guys are barking up the wrong tree. Forget about her. She has nothing to do with this. Seriously, believe me."

Agent Martin Williams said very forcefully, "We have very credible information, and we are going to interview this woman whether you want to come with us or not. If you know it, just give us the location that we should go to, otherwise, we can find her though our own means."

The local lawman stood up and pulled a cell phone from his right cargo pocket on his shorts.

"What are you doing?" barked Williams.

"Well, I am going to call JJ and tell her we are on the way."

"You will do no such thing!" Martin said even louder than before. "We do not warn suspects that we are coming, that's crazy!" Williams was convinced he was dealing with the least professional law enforcement officer imaginable.

JP sat down at his desk and started to stroke his goatee again, mumbling under his breath: "What's crazy is surprising JJ." He looked into space and said as if an audible comment to himself, "Guess I have to go and try to keep these guys out of trouble."

As all the FBI agents stood up, their host, Deputy Barnett, stayed seated, and continued to talk to himself out loud, "What about the dogs? Wonder if I should bring something."

Agent Betty Sato slowly moved towards the framed newspaper on the wall. After looking down in what appeared to be deep thought, she commented,. "Your father must be a very interesting man."

"You could say that." The deputy laughed a bit. "Very few people go out of their way to upset the French military with a personal submarine and risk being blown out of the water."

Sato responds, "That's not all is it? He makes 37.8 million dollars as a class action lawyer on one single case. Then disappears in the Caribbean for years, later ends up on the news for surfacing a submarine in the Sein River near the Eiffel Tower. Your father gets two officers in French intelligence fired, makes friends with the mayor of Paris and then opens a sandwich shop off the Champs-Élysées."

JP protests, "It's not exactly a sandwich shop, it's a super fancy restaurant with an insane selection of wine, live jazz, and gourmet sub-sandwiches," adding with a smile, "very expense sub-sandwiches. Plus, a famous mini-sub hanging from one wall."

Betty confirmed her knowledge of it: "La submarine Americana."

"Exactamont, and I suggest you call way ahead, there is a long list to get in," JP warned, with full knowledge that the agent had no intention of going.

Agent Williams headed for the door, saying, "Enough chit chat, let's roll." The other two FBI agents quickly followed.

JP took up the rear, followed by his dogs. As they passed down the hall the guests looked back, each wondering. *Does he think he's taking those pets with us?* Only agent George Gonzalez decided to actually ask, "You are not thinking of taking your poodles with us, are you?"

Both dogs flank the Latino agent at once: white one on the left, black on the right, baring their teeth and growling very slowly and deeply. From around the corner a few feet away Mary started laughing loudly.

JP quickly said, "Hey, Jorge my dogs think you look like a Mexican and that you are an illegal."

"Do not call me Jorge, and I am Cuban. I was born in Miami." The angry response from agent Gonzalez was exactly what deputy Barnett expected, as he knew full well George was Cuban.

JP had his return cued up: "Tu madre te llame Jorge." Then he added, "I know that, but my dogs do not. They are Barbet French water dogs, and they do not want to be called poodles anymore then you want them to call you a Mexican. So don't start exchanging insults you three."

The short-fit Latino seemed to get taller and even more muscular as he thought, *Why does he think he knows what my mother called me? My grandfather always told me to use my English name.* But before George could speak, Martin Williams ended it.

"Tone it down, now!" commanded the lead agent. Williams was thinking, *This stupid cracker is a racist. JP looks like an idiot. How did he get this job?*

The Barbets were still growling. JP said to George, "Just say you're sorry, please."

George responded, "Sorry?" That was good enough, as the canines did not recognize Gonzalez was asking a question, not apologizing. JP held out both hands towards the dogs, palms down. The deputy patted the air as the aggression stopped.

Deputy Barnett said, "I should have introduced you," bringing his right hand to his side. "This is Poivre." The black dog quickly came to JP's side. "And this is Sel." He was joined by the pure white K9 on his left.

Barbets normally are black or gray or chocolate brown, so Sel was very special, as she was pure white. Plus, she was big, sixty-five pounds, even larger than Poivre, although he was fairly large at fifty-eight lbs. French water dogs like these were not that easy to mistake for poodles, if you knew a little about dog breeds. Clearly Gonzalez was not a canine expert.

Martin was ready to get this show on the road. "Great, now we are all friends.", as he continued towards the front door of the Annex.

They all exited and JP called out "Mary, see you at the RC. We will be there at lunch."

# 2

# Visit the prime suspect

As soon as the entire "crew" stepped out the front door of the Annex, JP Barnett excitedly yelled, "Wow! A red Kia Soul. Very sporty! I thought the bureau made you guys drive black Suburbans - at least that's how it looks on TV."

Betty Sato quickly covered her mouth and suppressed a giggle while George Gonzalez turned away to hide his smile. Williams knew his team found this funny, as they had joked about it for 100 miles. Martin responded, "You watch too much TV, and that's all that Avis had in Orlando. We were conducting a seminar there when the Director personally called me and ask that I contact his old friend Sheriff Richardson. Once Agent Sato screened the tips, we were sent ASAP until the terrorist team from Langley gets here Monday."

JP said, "Sel, Poivre, and I have planned to solve this before Monday," as both dogs perked up looked super happy just at the mention of their names. "We should take my Jeep. JJ will not want to see such a sporty Red Kia blasting up her drive."

Seeing the hesitation from Williams, deputy Barnett reenforced his suggestion, "Seriously, it would be a good idea to drive up in a vehicle that she recognizes. Believe me."

"Ok, makes sense. Let's take your car," confirmed Williams.

Taking the lead across the Coastal highway, JP headed towards his small house right across A1A. Not just any street, A1A is the most famous road in Florida - straight down the east coast from Georgia to the Florida Keys. In West Palm Beach, a house on Highway A1A would be way over 10 million dollars. Delightfully, in Crescent Beach normal people with normal incomes can live, hang out, and play on this tropical ocean front route.

A yellow Jeep Wrangler 4-door was parked in front of the deputy JP Barnett's unassuming beach house. Actually, calling it a 4-door is taking some liberty, as all the doors had been removed, as had the top. But the tailgate was still there with a spare tire bolted to it. JP swung open that rear door and his dogs jumped in the back. Two biscuits were produced from a left cargo pocket and enthusiastically eaten.

George asked, "So you take these dogs everywhere?"

"Yes, always. These dogs are my partners." With that the deputy said, "Climb in, it's only a couple minutes away."

After brushing sand off the seat Sato took her seat behind JP, and the others just sat down with Williams in shotgun. Gonzalez in the rear to the right of Betty. As dirty and old as the Wrangler looked it fired right up and as soon as it was running JP looked down at the box between the front seats. Cassette tapes marked *Rock, Jazz, Blues, Mo-town,* etc., all turned with handwritten label up.

As Barnett picked out a tape, Williams thought, *Does this hick think I want to hear rhythm and blues because I'm black?* The tape that was stuck in the dash player was clearly marked R&B.

Then from directly behind the driver, Betty Sato said, "You know there are new, more modern ways to play music?"

This first of many friendly jabs was greeted with JP's response: "Digital music sounds like trash. Too much compression."

A large sound bar mounted to the roll bar accompanied sub-woofers on the top corners of the windshield ignited with a homemade instrumental of chimes, drums, acoustic bass, and something hard to ID. George Gonzales offered, "I like it, what is this?" as the Jeep jumped on to A1A and headed for the nearby bridge over the intercostal waterway.

"It's a cover of 'Sitting On the Dock of the Bay'," responded Williams.

After a bit of thought, the seemingly brilliant Betty Sato added, "The first posthumous single to ever hit the top of US charts. Recoded by Otis Redding days before his death in 1967."

Amazed and curious about Sato's knowledge, JP decided to let it slide and announced they were just now crossing the intercoastal and should be there soon. Betty continued to show off: "The intercostal waterway, a 3000-mile inland waterway running from Boston to Brownsville, Texas. Begun in 1826 and completed in 1949."

"OK, I GET IT, you're a walking encyclopedia, but can you sing and dance?" said JP as he quickly turned left and the Jeep sped down a dirt path lined with palms and crossed a small bridge.

Three otters looked up from the foot of the bridge and shambled for the water, just as Betty saw them and mused, "Awe, they are so cute, what are they?"

Amazed by agent Sato's comment and question, JP responded, "Well, they are otters, and they may look cute, but I wouldn't fool with them if I were you."

"Really? They look so fuzzy and friendly."

Deputy Barnett wondered how this serious FBI agent that seemed to know everything all of sudden sounded like a child just discovering the existence of otters. Then JP gave her the warning: "I know a woman that tried to pet a young one, and the mother otter didn't like that. Now that woman has two less fingers than normal."

The Jeep made two right turns on a narrow path lined by low growth palms and came to an abrupt stop in a small clearing about fifty yards in front of a tiny wooden house surrounded by a large porch. "We can walk from here," advised JP.

Everyone stepped out and Deputy Barnett went to the back of the Jeep to let his dogs out. Leaning over and petting each on the head, softly their master told them "Watch yourselves, take no risks." Like many dog owners, JP talked to the Barbets like they are people.

All six arrivals, four human, two canine, start to move towards the house. After walking up to the left of Martin for a better view, George looked hard twice and said, "Holy crap, that's an M21 SWS!"

Betty did not seem to take a close look but instead looked down for a second. She then gave more information: "The M21 Sniper Weapon System is the semi-automatic sniper rifle adaptation of the M14 rifle, chambered for the 7.62×51mm NATO cartridge and 7.62×54mmR for Vietnamese and Chinese modified versions."

Williams said, "Thank you, Agent Sato. But George and I know full well what it is and what it can do, in the right hands."

JP joked, "Well, I didn't know that. It is very helpful Betty. Now can you tell me what brand her boots are and what they were made out of?"

Instead of playing along with Deputy Barnett's nonsense, the FBI agents sized up the environment as they approached. Neither the woman on the porch in a wicker chair nor the bloodhound at her feet nor the wooden crate on the floor next to excited them. But the rifle sure got every agent's attention.

Getting close to the porch quicker than JP had planned, he said, "OK, just stay cool. Everything should be fine, I hope." Barnett took the lead and headed to the house, adding, "But if things go south, take out the dog first."

Sel and Poivre made no sound but stuck close to their master, the entire group continuing to move forward at a pace that might have been too quick. Oswald, the bloodhound, raised his head and then went back to looking like he was asleep. Laughingly, George Gonzalez asked, "That dog?"

A tall woman with a short gray hair wearing very faded overalls with a white t-shirt underneath and large brown army boots stood up. George instinctively moved his right hand towards his rear holster, the guests still moving forward at a faster clip.

The woman on the porch whistled and called out a single word: "Lobo."

A rather large Alaskan grey wolf appeared from the right side of the house. Seeing the group, the predator bared his teeth and started a low auditable warning. The Barbets moved apart about 10 feet - white to the left and black to the right, as if they were executing a tactic — which in fact they were.

JP turned to George and said, "That dog!"

"Oh my god, that's no dog!!" exclaimed Betty Sato.

A voice rang out from the house. "JP, I cannot guarantee that Lobo and your French puppies will not get into it." This advice was a backhanded way of pointing out that even two well trained large Barbets would likely fail at defending themself against any grey wolf. And Lobo was not just any grey wolf!

JP put both his arms out and patted the air, then moved his hands to his legs. Sel and Poivre moved in, one on each side. Slowly Barnett turned around and pointed towards the Jeep. "Aller!" His dogs slowly backed up in unison while keeping a sharp eye on the grey wolf. Again, JP commanded, "Aller." Instantly one black and one white streak appeared and within seconds Barnett's dogs where in his Wrangler. Sometimes animals have better instincts than humans.

George said, "That looks like a grey wolf." To which the owner yelled back from the porch, "A Yukon grey wolf, that is not fond of visitors."

Betty was totally taken aback but after a little thought, she did her thing again: "The Yukon grey or Alaskan grey wolf has a normal range in British Columbia, the northwest territory and Alaska, with weights for females of 85 lbs and males of 130." Then Betty asked, "Are you sure that is a Yukon grey?"

The woman yelled back: "YES, I am sure. Lobo is big for his breed because I keep feeding him unwanted guests!" She was not kidding about the size. At 180 lbs Lobo might have been the largest Yukon grey on record (maybe she was kidding about the feeding him guests).

As the visitors slowly continued to walk towards the house, JP said, "I am sorry to surprise you JJ, but these folks just want to speak to you for a minute."

JJ Cormack, who clearly thought she was being intruded on, screamed, "YOU COULD HAVE CALLED ME, JP!"

Deputy Barnett started to explain, "Well, I wanted to, but..."

The woman interrupted, "BUT the FBI told you not to. Since when do you take orders from the feds?"

All three agents looked surprised and then turned to JP, wondering how this suspect knew they were with the bureau. Seeing him being visually accused, JJ said,"NO, he didn't sneak me a message. You people look just like what you are, unless that little one is really a robot. Hmmm, yes, she could be a Chinese robot."

Betty defended herself before her boss got to it: "First, I am Japanese, and second, you mean 'android,' not 'robot.'" Sato thought to herself, *I am so tired of playing the inscrutable soulless automaton. Someday I will breakout and they will all see my passion, maybe not today or this week or this year, but someday.*

JJ laughed. "Good, she has emotions." Then she turned to JP and said, "YOU owe my dogs three birds, for your uninvited visit." And JJ pointed over her head and to the right.

Across an inlet by the far shore, a couple dozen egrets were standing knee deep in the water.

JP had to object. "Even if I hit one, the others will be gone before I get a second, and why three?"

Holding up three fingers, JJ demanded, "And it better be head shots. I do not want my dogs getting lead poisoning.  And Lobo is a growing boy and deserves two."

Agent Martin Williams was thinking, *I am not surprised this cracker has his pistol in his boot* as JP bent over and produced a .38 revolver from his foot wear.

George challenged the deputy, "I will bet you don't get one, much less three."

JP thought, *Who is this guy to judge me without seeing if I can shoot?* Of course, he knew Gonzalez was likely right, as JP said, "Oh yeah, I suppose you can do better?" To which the dare was almost answered, as Gonzalez reached behind his back to produce his Glock Gen 5.

The FBI team leader broke his silence. "Agent Gonzalez, discharge that service weapon and you will have to file a 537A."

The Glock went back in place, just as Betty Sato excitedly said, "I need to point out…" when she was rudely interrupted by the suspect.

JJ yelled, "HOLD ON BABE, I got to see this" as the woman on the porch turned and bent over the box by her side. Picking up two items, JJ marched quickly towards the group. As one item was clearly a gun, Betty stopped speaking and reached under her coat, but the female agent was stopped by the large hand of Martin on her arm.

The tall woman in overalls walked straight up to Gonzalez: "Here, chico," handing him a Ruger Mark IV. "You won't have to file a freakin report if you use this, and in case you need a bit more time," she held out in her other hand a six-inch screw-in silencer.

George Gonzalez assured her, "I will not need an edge." The Cuban took the Ruger, and bounced it in his hand as if he was weighing it. Then he stepped to the left a few paces and looked at the birds.

Sato repeated, "I need to point out-" and this time she was interrupted by her boss, Martin Williams: "Shhh, I GOTTA SEE THIS."

*Bang,* no bird flew. *Bang Bang,* two birds lost their heads. *Bang,* all the birds started to fly and finally the fifth *Bang,* and a third egret was decapitated mid-flight.

JJ yelped, "Yee Haa, that's good."

Agent Williams turned to the shooter. "That's five shots for three birds. Are you losing it, George? "

"The sights are off," came the excuse, from the guy everyone in the agency knew was the best shot in the FBI.

With a serious expression, Williams said, "Maybe that explains the first miss, but two?"

By now Betty got the joke and covered her mouth as she laughed and tried to say straight faced, "Yes, maybe more time on the practice range," but she was giggling so much it was hard to decipher what's being said.

"What? Are you ..." then Gonzalez broke off, realizing it's a joke. George thought about his grandfather for a second time today. He recalled being taken every day starting at age six to an orange grove in Dade County where his abuelo worked. And he was shown how to load and shoot that single shot bolt action .22 riffle he got at his sixth Christmas. Same rifle every day, every summer, just smaller and further targets until he was 14, when grandpa handed him a Colt .45 and said, "This was my brother's, and I hope you become the man Castro fears." Of course, George knew what his grandfather would never admit: ex-pat Cubans in South Florida would never take Cuba back from the communists.

Williams looked very closely at JJ for just a bit too long and turned his head to Betty. "Now, Agent Sato, what do you need to point out?"

"The common egret is also known as the great egret, or large egret, or great white heron, normally about one meter tall, with wing span of almost two meters but weighing only about one kilo , and..."

Martin interrupted Sato: "What's the point?"

Betty moved to the punch line in a very low tone: "Egrets are protected under the Federal Migratory Bird Act."

To which JP started laughing.

JJ turned and pointed in the direction of the water, yelling, "Lobo dinner, Oswald dinner." Then, as she turned to the group and was about to comment that dogs cannot be arrested for eating evidence, the woman in overalls was shocked as Special Agent Martin Williams stepped forward and said directly in her face, "I know you. You're Jackie Hamilton "

# 3

# Who is this woman?

The tall older grey-headed woman, who thought she was past being surprised, looked closely at Agent Williams. She just shook her head and turned to walk the three steps up and back onto her porch.

Williams followed, and when JJ turned around, he was in her comfort zone. Martin slowly put out his hand to gently grasp her waist. Most men would have gotten a rude surprise as a response. However, JJ looked down and saw the bottom of a familiar tattoo revealed as the agent's shirt sleeve moved up at the extension of his arm. "You... you … were too young to be there. How do you know that name?"

Williams quickly turned around as he sensed his colleagues approaching, the special agent making a motion to back up with his hand. Martin meant to ensure a private conversation. JP, George, and Betty all got the message and backed off. Softly Martin said as he turned back to JJ, "I studied Section 8s at Quantico."

The woman stared at Williams speechless, as the ex-marine, now FBI agent, continued, "Of course, the case of a Marine nurse, the hero of a surprise firefight, suddenly walking into the middle of camp naked while firing a pistol in the air, is rather unusual."

"Please don't call me Jackie."

Williams nodded reassuringly. Somehow there seemed to be a bond growing already.

Oswald and his reminder of his ancestors walked up to the edge of the house, well fed and still slightly wet. Lobo instinctively growled. Three people at ground level tensed up a bit and moved back from the house a few feet before JJ could point to the rear and shout "Back!" to which the canines quickly disappeared.

Although Sato could not hear her boss and the suspect, as they were speaking very softly, she saw JJ pick up the sniper riffle and hand it to Williams. Betty was glad to see that and said to JP and George, "Good, Martin is disarming her."

JP looked at Sato and smiled in a way that clearly conveyed: "AS IF!"

Williams looked closely at the weapon and cocked it, ejecting a round. Still low and out of earshot to the others, the agent said, "You keep it loaded and off safety."

JJ smiled back. "Doesn't do much good empty and not ready."

Martin was intrigued: "JJ, I really want to understand what happened."

"Why?" responded the woman that the military had concluded was no longer mentally fit to serve.

"Honestly, between us, my father went through basically the same thing." Williams paused before adding, "And then there are those rumors of the 'angel of death.'"

JJ seemed to be thinking a bit, then responded, "Wars create lots of rumors, you know that." She looked up as if to remember some examples. "Like gremlins. Do you really think strange animals actually jumped on planes in WW2 and sabotaged them mid-flight?"

"I know what you mean. My favorite is how the British press thought Ben Franklin had traveled to France during the revolution to build a lightning collector that could be used to blow up Great Britain from across the English Channel."

"Really? That's wild." JJ's eyes widened and a childish curiosity seemed to fill her face.

Williams said, "Yep, amazing, isn't it? About as likely as a super tall woman running around randomly shooting high-level Vietcong from as far away as three klicks."

"See, that would be a couple of miles. Sounds like a fog of war rumor to me."

"Can I ask how you ended up naked and acting in such an unexplainable way that day?"

The once-respected nurse and soldier took a long look into her inquisitors' eyes then reached out and ran her hand up his left arm, revealing the complete tattoo. After a long silence JJ softly said, "I left Tyler, Texas on April 7th after my little brother, Luke, begged me to stay. He was only eight, and that kid had the clearest blue eyes on earth. When I looked into his eyes, I felt I could see the infinity of existence."

JJ took a deep breath and looked up for a long time, then she moved in closer and stared straight into Williams' face before continuing, "Then November 1, 1966 I was called in by the C.O. and told Luke had been accidentally shot by a friend. I kind of lost it. The entire next month was a blur until I received a letter and record from Texas that Luke had sent a few days before Halloween. It took a month for me to get something mailed from Tyler. I found a record player and listened to this 45 several hundred times until, on Dec 1st, I finally snapped. That's all I can say about it. "

"What was the record?" asked Martin very sympathetically.

JJ looked like she might cry, then straightened up. "'Universal Soldier' by Buffy Saint Marie."

Williams was honestly moved, and wanted to relay his feelings the best he could. "I will not ask what the letter said. That is between you and Luke."

Clearly wanting to go back to trying to forget all this shit, JJ just said, "Thanks."

Martin wanted to know more, but understood he should not ask directly, so, he just commented, "You know, November 1966 I recall is when Hathcock took out the Vietcong sniper called Apache."

"Did he?" asked JJ with a slight grin.

"By all accounts, yes. But around that time there were those rumors of that angel of death," said Martin.

JJ had to head this off before it went too far: "Let's not talk about old rumors. Let's get to your reason to visit me."

Williams looked from side to side and then back at his companions, who were standing and talking about lunch. At least JP and George were discussing sandwiches, while Betty stared at her phone. Trying to gracefully change the topic, Martin observed, "You seem to like the throw," pointing at the round wooden target at the far end of the porch.

"You could say that," JJ said as she walked to the target and pulled out four bladed throwing knifes. With a lively step in her walk back, she handed one of the weapons to Martin.

Williams inspected it closely, turning it over slowly in his hand. A straight piece of stainless steel with no handle per se, shaped for only one purpose. An object he could admire but had never been able to master. The special agent observed, "This is a Randall pro-thrower. These are really expensive knives. I am no expert, but I know Randall makes the best. I have a friend who waited 18 months to get one."

JJ responded with a little pride, "Actually these are not exactly the pro-thrower model. These were made custom for me. The company supplies them to me for the Blade Show." She took back the object of interest, as JP called out, "Can we join the party?"

Deputy Barnett yelled to the woman with four blades in her hand, "Roger told me he made you a special target, and if you are doing a demo, I want to watch." JJ looked at her guests, then she looked towards the target: two feet in diameter, wooden and painted in eight pie shaped slices, alternating red and blue in color. The disc was mounted to a tripod wooden stand. Then JJ said, "The Blade Show in Atlanta is not till June, so I am may not be completely ready. But what the shit, I will give it a try."

As the strays arrived at the steps to the porch, George said softy to JP, "A target that size from twenty feet seems kind of tame for the Blade Show. Kids in their back yard can do that."

JP looked over at his new foodie friend and whispered, "Wait."

Being a part time employee of the most famous knife maker on earth was a privilege that JJ took seriously. With a determined look, she reached in her overalls' front pocket and produced a small black controller, which JJ handed to Martin. "Green button to start, red one to stop. Start when I nod." Then turning to the group, the lady holding the knives said, "Hey, Robot, pick a color."

Betty said only, "What?"

"Red or blue, just pick one," yelled the woman in overalls and army boots.

Sato said loudly, with a bit of irritation in her voice, "BLUE."

JJ smiled and stepped away from the target a few more feet and freezes with her feet apart and solidly planted. She put two blades between her teeth: one headed east, the other west. The two other blades, one in each hand, were gripped by the business end.

Turning to the control handler, JJ moved her head up and down slightly. Williams hit the green button and the target began to spin at a slow but increasing rate. Just as the disc began to turn purple, the sound of impact rang out, and everyone looked away from the target back at the thrower as JJ grabbed the remaining two knives from her mouth. Quicker than the observers could process, another impact.

As Williams pushed the red button, JJ turned away from the target and held her head down and lowly said, "Crap." Like a bowler who knows when the ball leaves their grasp that it's not exactly right, she sensed that more practice was needed before June, especially if she was to get a bonus. Last year her demo of how to bounce a knife off two parallel walls and still hit a bullseye got JJ $5000 in extra pay.

As the disc slowed, George yelled in a distinctively NOT FBI fashion, "Holy crap." JP looked at him and put two hands palms up shoulder high and tilted his head to one side: "Kids in the back yard?"

Two blades were in the dead center of two opposite blue pie slices, but two others were splitting the edges where the two blue slices met red.

As JJ turned back around to view her work, Martin said, "Very impressive. I know by June you will be perfect and beyond amazing." Williams knew exactly the type of woman he was facing, just as he knew how much agent Betty Sato had messed up.

Sato, with no emotion, asked, "Now, can we get to the matter of local terror?"

Betty's boss gave her a look that made her blood run cold and pointed toward the Jeep. "I will meet both of you back in the vehicle. We are through here." Watching as Betty and George head back as directed, then turning to JJ, the special agent continues, "I have only one question, JJ: do you know anything that can help us with the strange events going on here in Crescent Beach?"

Slowly looking at both men, Martin and JP, and then focusing on her old friend, she said, "I know that JP will find whichever crazy witch is messing with our town and take her out." Turning back to Williams, JJ said, "I really do not want to offend you, but we all have faith that our guy will end this soon."

"Nothing else that can help us?" asked Williams.

JJ shook her head. Then she looked at JP and softly asked, "How is he? He could stay here. It's safe."

Deputy Barnett reassured her, "I know. He's good, and I will not let you down."

Williams held out his hand and received a shake that was as firm as he'd imagined, as he thought, *How did my team get suckered into this so-called lead? This is an embarrassment. Who could think Jackie Hamilton would do these things? If this woman wanted to cause trouble, people would be dead. I bet she could hit that target from over a mile away with the M21, even today. This is on Sato. I counted on her.*

Martin wanted to say more to JJ, but just turned and headed down the steps.

# 4

## Rooftop sniper

As George and Betty neared the Wrangler, the Barbets jump from their position in the rear over the seatback to the storage area. Williams and JP were a few yards back, and Williams yelled as his juniors reached the vehicle, "Agent Sato!"

Turning around, phone in hand, Betty stopped typing. "Yes, sir."

JP couldn't help but think, *Her hands are so small, and that phone looks so big. Plus, why is it three times as thick as most phones? Maybe it is a special Fed phone where they pay ten times normal price due to it being supplied by some company that has an ex-general or son of a senator on the board of directors.*

Williams was as direct as you might guess: "Agent Sato, I want to know what the hell just went on there. It's your job to find out! Clearly these solid leads were BS, and it was a waste of time."

"Sir, with all due respect, I could not hear your discussion with the suspect and…"

Interrupting Sato, who clearly was not getting to the point, he said, "Use your head. She was never a suspect. Do you think Jackie Hamilton would use a .22 rifle and try to kill people and miss? Look that up!"

Betty Sato responded, "Sir, I have not found her record yet. There seem to be 75,678 people named Jackie

Hamilton in the USA, with over 12,000 in Florida. Many of those could be men."

Williams continued to be frustrated with this embarrassing waste of time: "Forget it. The point here is: who called in multiple false tips? Find that out!"

Agent Sato agreed. "Yes, sir! It could take till Monday." JP was not very comfortable with this or any tense discussion, so he threw in, "By Monday it will be over. But right now, George and I have an important appointment with a sandwich." Special Agent Williams was wondering why this strange excuse for a deputy thought the case would be solved that soon. And what's with the appointment with a sandwich?

The team of sleuths quickly moved into the Wrangler. Its pilot cranked it up and bent over and pulled hard on one of two long aftermarket levers to the left of the driver's seat. Dropped it into first and floored it, with right wheels locked, the Jeep spinning around in place on the dirt road.

Surprised by how close the palms that lined the trail came to his face in the maneuver, George let out an excited, "Whoa." Unphased by the vegetation that almost slapped his face, Williams said, "It's too early for lunch. I want to see the spot where the sniper shot from."

The driver said, "Great, that's right on the way to the RC, and it will only take a minute." JP drove with a seeming sense of urgency. "Lunch on Friday is always fabulous. Frenchie makes his take on a Cuban with plantain chips."

As they crossed back over the intercoastal, Deputy Barnett noticed something under the bridge and said, "I need one quick sidetrack."

Whipping the Jeep down a dirt trail right past the bridge, JP abruptly stopped alongside three bikes that laid beside a thick grove of palms. Barnett got out and screamed, "Billy! Billy Giles, get up here right now."

A teenage boy with extra curly blonde hair sheepishly slow walked up to the trail from the banks of the intercoastal. "Hey, JP."

"It's a school day and you are down here with Ivan and Roy, fishing and getting stoned. What do you think I should do about that?" The boy just stared, then started to speak.

Barnett knew there would be no sensible answer, so he just said, "Wait, never mind, hand me your phone." Once in hand, it was returned with a forceful demand: "Unlock it."

Billy complied and JP took the phone and began to type.

"I am entering my contact info, for a phone I use on this special case I have. I will text you what I want you to do. And I want you to find Andrew Chen, tell him I want him to help you, Ivan, and Roy with a special assignment I have for you."

"Andrew? He's a geek," responded the kid.

"Billy, just do what I am telling you to. You might find Andrew very helpful. You got this?" JP looked closely at the half-baked kid and added, "And I will be contacting

Andrew too, to make sure you are working with him. Got it?"

"Yeah" was all Billy had to say.

The deputy continued, "By the way, I am going to give you boys a code team name. I will call your team the 'The A1A Irregulars.'"

Billy just nodded. He didn't get it, but he felt good that JP was not causing a stink over skipping and stuff. But moreover, Billy was proud that the deputy seemed to want his help. Billy's parents never put any faith in him, and being a special assistant to a man like JP Barnett with a code team name made him have a feeling that he was completely unaccustomed to.

Once JP was back in the Wrangler, Martin commented, "Is that how you handle illegal drug use here? I could smell the weed from here. You couldn't have missed that."

"Are you with the DEA or the FBI?" chided the deputy.

Williams informed the local unprofessional clown, "The bureau is concerned with all violations of federal laws "

JP asked, "Really? Well, there are tons of retail and medical locations all over Florida and several other states that you need to get after ASAP." As deputy Barnett noticed the attitude forming in the face of Williams, he decided, *Why not have even more fun?* "You didn't seem too interested in whether that silencer that screws into that Ruger was registered, or that George murdered three PROTECTED birds. Do you not ever help the ATF or the US Fish and Wildlife Service? Which agency should you be calling first on those two things? Or were you just too distracted by the gun's owner?"

No response and no comment from anyone, as JP did another pit maneuver, but this time with the other wheels locked. They were speeding south on A1A in seconds. Within a mile, the Jeep pulled up alongside a small wooden building with "Cat and Moon Yoga" painted on the front door in bright red letters. And of course, there was also a logo on the sign of a feline in a full moon.

"Come on, let's look at the snipers spot, then we can get lunch," JP said as he jumped out and headed for a metal ladder that was bolted to the side of the two-story building. Barnett pulled down the lower extension saying, "Let's go."

The three FBI agents ascended in order by rank, which gave Barnett a perfect view of Betty as he followed them up. Once on the flat roof, covered with tar and gravel, the deputy marched straight to the front of the building and faced the beach, which lay fifty yards on the other side of the ocean road. "This is where I found the gun, the casings and a lipstick. As you might know by now, it was a Henry .22 lever action."

Betty inquired, "Have you been able to trace the serial number on the rifle?"

Always the smartass, JP looked surprised and asked, "Oh, do guns have serial numbers?"

Three sets of eyes rolled.

"OK, I didn't trace the number."

Three agents thought at once, *What's wrong with this idiot?*

JP decided to let them ask. However, the question he expected did not come. Instead, Williams made the easy connection. "So, you already knew the gun and who owned it? Tell us the entire circumstances in order."

Barnett started the story: "Well, I remember it all well, like it was just last Wednesday. Oh wait, it was just last Wednesday." And three sets of eyes rolled, again. "Anyway, I am in the front office talking to Hank about his truck being broken into. Maria and Hector rush in and Maria starts yelling that Hector has been shot."

JP pointed to his left forearm. "Seems Hector had been hit about here, and he was holding his arm and blood was dipping out between his fingers. Instantly, Mary pulls the first aid kit out of her desk and starts looking at Hector's arm. I ask Maria what happened."

The local deputy played with his goatee, then said, "Seems after talking to Maria and going to the beach, turns out a beach ball had been shot, and Fred Fox's sailboat had been hit two times. And it looked like one shot had ricocheted off the mast and hit Hector. Fred had sailed down to pass out cards promoting his party boat to the tourists, and he was kind of pissed that one shot had gone through a lower window and the sailboat was taking on water. I told him that... "

Martin did not have the patience for nonstop storytelling and interrupted: "Can you get to the point, seriously?"

"Well, I was getting to that. No need to run a trace. The Henry and some ammo had been stolen out of Hank's truck. Hank was standing in the Annex when the shooting happened. Being a brilliant detective, I deduced he wasn't the shooter."

"Did you hear the shots?" inquired Betty.

Laughing a bit, the deputy responded in detail: "It's a freaking .22. I maybe would hear it if I was standing next to the shooter. But from across the street and inside a building, really? And to answer your next question, no one heard the shots. But Rainbow, the owner of the yoga studio, heard the ladder being rattled. She went out and thought kids had been up on the roof again, went up to check and found the rifle, casings, and lipstick. Strangely a full box of .22 ammo was stolen, but it was not left."

"Is Rainbow a real name?" Betty asked as she smiled. "What about fingerprints, on the gun, the casings, the lipstick?"

"Fingers leave prints? Like an otter's feet on a mud bank?" quipped JP.

"STOP IT." Williams was getting noticeably pissed at JP's ongoing BS.

The deputy got the message. "Sorry, of course, I checked. And Rainbow does have a funny name, but her parents are hippies. But she did have the presence of mind to have not touched anything. The Henry had no prints, casings no prints, and the lipstick was covered with prints. But oddly, completely clean on the top and bottom of the tube. So, it was clear to me, the shooter left no prints." Then looking directly at Williams, "And I must say without regard to her strange name, Rainbow has ways to loosen people up, in case anyone feels a bit too tightly wound."

Martin skipped the advice about yoga and got back to business. "Did you run the prints on the lipstick through the system? Get any hits?"

"Yes, and yes, I know who owned the lipstick. She's not a suspect. I can go over that later if you like. But now, if you've seen enough, let's go to lunch," said JP, and turning to George, asked, "Ready to be shocked?"

George nodded yes and headed for the ladder, the other two agents look at each other and heading for the edge of the roof and the only exit, short of jumping off, which likely only Betty could do without being hurt.

# 5

## George recalls Bahia de Cochinos

Back at sea level, everyone took their standard Jeep sitting. As JP inserted the key, he saw a large hand grab his right arm as Martin asked, "Can we turn around in a more normal fashion?"

The deputy gave in. "Your wish is my command, but I must point out that normality is overrated."

To which Williams offered his professional view: "I should point out, there are plenty of amusement rides in Orlando. I could have stayed there if that was what I wanted."

JP dutifully turned the vehicle around and started to enter A1A, the famous seaside highway. Looking left, Barnett saw three young girls headed down the sidewalk on skateboards. As he waited, they all rode by slowly.

The lead girl yelled, "Hola, amigo" and the other two started to wave and laugh.

"Go, birds, go," was the reply from the driver.

The last skater yelled back, "We will be ready, Mr. JP."

Williams thought, *What is with this guy? No one has called girls 'birds' since the 60s. Come to think of it, maybe this idiot is stuck in some kind of time warp.*

After heading south, the Jeep had only a few blocks to go before turning west on a two-lane residential road. A few small frame houses on each side, unkept yards, with the occasional lawn decorations: pink flamingos, plastic dolphins, and such. Each house with several palm trees, some short and a few very tall.

At the end of the road sat a barricade with two concrete poles on each side and three rusted steel planks decorated with red reflectors, even though anyone could easily see the intercoastal waterway was dead ahead. Right before the warning, a small gravel driveway led to the front of what appeared to be a large wooden southern style two-story house, painted yellow and white, with wrap around porch on both floors, and wide wooden steps leading up to the first-floor porch. Over the steps a six-foot wide, four-foot-tall light blue sign with black letters.

"'The Raven Conspiracy,'" Betty Sato read out loud. "That's an odd name "

JP responded, "It's a great name and even better restaurant. The name is from the grouping, like a herd of cattle."

"Or swarm of bees," the granddaughter of a Japanese beekeeper threw in.

JP wanted to keep this game going. "Caravan of camels."

"Cloud of bats." Betty was not going to be last to list.

"Quiver of cobras," returned the deputy.

"Parade of elephants," from the back seat.

"School of fish." JP had to admit to himself he was running thin and had to retreat to the standards.

"Shiver of sharks." Going in for the kill in this contest, Betty doubled down. "Pandemonium of parrots."

Already out of Jeep, Williams and Gonzalez were ready to stop this nonsense. George said, "Let's eat."

JP had to throw in, "And my favorite, a murder of crows," as he disembarked.

"My favorite is an army of frogs," Sato said, smiling almost childishly. "And they are so…" then Betty stopped mid-sentence, realizing she was about to sound like she looked.

The men didn't notice, or if they did, they didn't show it. All three guys were making their way up the wooden stairs. Agent Williams barely cleared the bottom of the sign hanging in their path. He ducked down a little just to be sure, then, standing aside like a gentleman, he let the others enter first. The Barbets had leaped over the back seat and rushed through the door as it was held open.

Williams heard a few voices cry out "Hi, JP" and similar salutations from assorted people. He paid no attention. Martin first took time to size the place up, as always. Large open room that had clearly been several smaller ones before the walls were taken down, typical wooden high-top bar on the left running back thirty feet or so. This had been a large house. Dining area with assorted mixed design wooden tables and chairs, out of place staircase with white banisters on each side leading to the second floor. The access was blocked by a thick nautical looking rope. Past the stairs and not completely in clear view, another room with a pool table and lighting that indicated it had much higher ceilings than the main room. Sel and Poivre had taken their place laying under the gaming table next to two water bowls - one white and the other black.

At the end of the bar, a large black metal bird cage hung at the end of a curved metal hook which was part of a heavy black floor stand. On the bottom front side of the cage hung a gold-colored sign with the word "EDGAR" written on it in black lettering. Agent Williams of course recognized the Common Raven in the cage, who must be named Edgar. What he did not know was, this was not the original Edgar, who was a much better trained bird.

Everyone loved the original Edgar, who was allowed to fly free around the restaurant twice a day for about three minutes, once at 12:30 and once at 7:30. One day the bartender, Sam, forgot to lock the front door at 12:25 as he was instructed to do daily. A tourist pulled the door open at 12:31. Original Edgar AND Sam were never seen again in the RC. Now the new Edgar stayed in his cage.

The last item of real interest that Williams and both his team members noticed was over a door in the rear that likely led to the kitchen. There was a large American flag, and to the left a large portrait of Elvis. To the right was an equally sized one of JFK.

Even though they seemed strange for an eatery in 2020, only George thought about the pictures a lot. Gonzalez couldn't help but have a flood of feelings when seeing President Kennedy on the wall: the third time today he'd had memories of his grandfather. "Never forget George, Kennedy promised air cover at Bahia de Cochinos, and my brother died in front of my own eyes. You must promise me you will never vote for a Democrat. If it was Eisenhower who made that promise, my brother would be alive and Cuba would be free. I hate what they did."

Of course, Agent Gonzalez knew not all Democrats could be blamed for the Bay of Pigs and that broken promise. He also knew it was easiest to get along by never discussing politics, certainly a challenge in DC. But he would ever break his word to his beloved grandfather, nor would George forget what happened to his family.

As Williams followed the group towards a table that JP had already picked out, he noticed there were already several customers sitting solo at the bar. Through the dining area he passed one 4-top table with four older ladies playing what was probably bridge. Next table, four men that he studied closely. He knew their type. Martin decided then and there to preempt their inevitable questions.

Once arriving at the chosen table, all four were met by the owner. JP said, "Agent Williams, I want to introduce you to our host, Donna Reed." Barnett smiled and winked, which Martin found strange, but not nearly as much as the name and appearance of this woman. Average height but rather thin for a mid-thirties' mom type, blonde helmet hair parted in the middle with a big curl at the bottom right above the shoulders. And Donna's outfit was out of place, a cotton dress with two wide straps over the shoulders, form fitting down to the hips then flared out in with pleats until ending mid-calf. The patent leather skinny black shoes were the final touch. This woman looked like a late '50s / early '60s stereotype.

As he extended his hand he noticed the background music. 'What's that? The Everly Brothers' 'Bye Bye Love'?" Special Agent Williams thought, *This place is crazy. I need to solve this case and get back to DC.*

Donna shook each FBI agent's hand very very lightly while barely touching it, as JP made the rounds. Then Barnett confirmed what he already knew: "Donna, still the French-Cuban with plantains on Friday?"

"Oh, dear boy, of course. Frenchie would never change that without letting you know."

JP sat down, followed by the two junior agents, and he ordered. "We'll take four with ice teas."

Williams, still standing, said, "I'll be right back" as he turned and walked back to the table with four men. Betty got up and followed a couple of feet behind her boss.

The two left behind had more important matters to discuss. JP started with, "George, I do not want to insult your mother or grandmother or whoever, but you have never had a Cuban sandwich like this, and may I say, not nearly as good."

Agent Gonzalez felt he should follow his colleagues, but couldn't resist talking about food with JP. "It will have to be very good. My grandmother made the best one I have ever had. She slowed roasted the pork for 24 hours at really low temperature. You cannot believe how tender."

Arriving at his target, Williams looked down at the four men. "You guys are reporters, and I want to let you know how this will go down. I am Special Agent Martin J. Williams with the FBI. When I have news for you, I will text or call you and let you know. There will be no press conference or following us around." Giving each man a close look in turn, Martin continued, "Please give me your cards and I will be in touch when we have something."

The oldest and least well-kept sounded in first, "Kelly Ford, *Atlanta Journal Constitution.*" He reached for his wallet and pulled out a card, handing it over. He said, "That second number is my cell." By the time Kelly had gotten his card out, the other three had produced their cards and handed them over. "James Fabella, *Miami Herald,*" said the most senior reporter. "That's Eric McKee from *Tampa Bay Times.* He used to work with me on the Gold Coast beat." Last, a very young-looking guy in jeans and a t-shirt said, "Vincent Bravo, *New York Times.*"

Williams looked at the last reporter closely, then observed, "I am surprised the *Times* is here."

Bravo responded, "I was on a vacation, just down to visit my grandparents in Palm Coast, when I heard about the action here. My boss said I should pick up whatever I could while I am in the area."

Sliding the cards into his inner coat pocket, Williams just made a casual salute, turned and walked back to the table, Betty in tow. Once back and seated, Agent Sato said, "It is funny that all four of those reporters have facial hair. The old guy has a full beard, two others unshaven for days, and the *New York Times* guy has a perfect goatee."

JP observed, "A little bit too perfect for my taste" as he stroked his own goatee. "A pack of wolves, that's what those guys are. I had already asked them to not interfere twice. I hope you guys reinforced that."

"A prickle of porcupines." Betty thought that the deputy was starting the challenge over by using the term 'pack of wolves.'

The lead agent was over this BS. "Stop it! seriously, let's hear about the other two attacks."

Just then Donna walked up with a tray with four plates, sitting each by the iced teas she had delivered earlier. "Enjoy your lunch. Let me know if you need anything else."

Sato was the first to comment about what all three Feds were thinking, "This is unusual. We didn't get menus to order. They just bring what they want?"

JP explained, "It is unusual, I agree. But this is not a typical restaurant. Frenchie only fixes one dish per meal. Well except at Sunday brunch."

Donna had put down four white plates that looked exactly alike, a baguette opened with thinly sliced ham, topped with Swiss cheese, with pulled pork piled on top. To the side were a stack of crisp plantain chips, a small ramekin of speckled mustard and a pickle. Without comment George and JP both picked up their sandwich and went to work.

"Oh my god! This is fantastic. What the hell? This pork is crazy good," was the first thing out of the Latino's mouth after the beginning bite.

Both the other agents looked at George after his spontaneous outburst. His boss said, "Agent Gonzalez, stay cool."

Attempting to be professional and explaining himself at the same time, Gonzalez said, "Try it, and see."

Martin picked up his Cuban sandwich and took a bite while Betty just picked up a chip and nibbled on it, then quickly had another. Surprised, the extra-small female agent said, "These chips are not oily at all. Is this a type of banana?"

George laughed and shook his head while JP just wondered, *What's with this woman? Knows everything and nothing at the same time.*

Agent Williams, after finishing his second bite, observed, "The pork is very good, and the bread is like the kind I used to get in New Orleans. I cannot completely figure out the pork marinade. Hint of orange and cayenne, but there is something else."

JP added, "How about we just enjoy our lunch and talk about the case when we leave?" Everyone made a 'um hum' sound, as it would be way too impolite to respond otherwise with mouths stuffed.

Donna returned with a new plate holding two large soup bones. "May I?" she whispered as she leaned in close to JP's ear. After receiving the OK, that Donna knew would come, she literally skipped over to the Barbets and presented their treat. Not many adults actually skip these days. Maybe more should.

As he finished his lunch, Williams cast his eyes around the RC. "Is that the local postman?" Martin asked, tilting his head towards a skinny guy at the bar in traditional bluish gray shirt and shorts with standard postal emblem on the right sleeve.

The local deputy responded after finishing a chip he was enjoying. "Well spotted, Sherlock. That's Zen Buckner. He has been delivering the mail here forever."

Not entertained by the Sherlock comment, Martin observed, "Hmmm, I have seen him drink two beers, and it looks like he is getting a third."

JP got his drift and responded, "So you are with the USPS now? Seriously, he's a great guy, so what if he likes beer?"

"The so what is, the government does not pay people to get wasted on the job."

"Really? You could have fooled me! Ever watch C-SPAN? The entire congress acts like they are drunk or worse. In fact…"

Williams interrupted before he had to sit through the local numbskull degrading the federal government. "OK, I got it. It's not your problem. Let's get to the matter at hand."

JP just stood up and headed for the door. Within seconds Sel and Poivre dropped their bones and were on his heels. Turning around he yelled back, "Donna, put this on my tab, thanks."

As Donna responded, "You got it, have a great day."

Williams was thinking, *This guy probably eats free everyday by doing favors for businesses. Corruption is likely worse in these hick towns than in New York or Chicago.*

Once the door was opened, a white and a black blur passed by JP as he shouted his best John Wayne imitation: "Come on, pilgrims, we are burning daylight."

# 6

## Drive to the Old Town

Once all the sleuths and dogs were loaded up in the Wrangler, JP turned to his right. "What now, chief?"

Williams pulled a small black notebook from inside his suit coat and said, "I would like to talk to Carol Blink."

Deputy JP Barnett was not down with the idea of Carol being questioned by this guy. "Why? I can tell you all she knows, plus, she's still in the hospital and I do not want her upset any more than she already is." Barnett felt very bad about what happened to Carol on his watch. He truly wanted to protect and help her, if he could.

"My team will interview Ms. Blink with or without you."

"I will definitely be there. She's in Flagler hospital, so it'll be a short ride"

"How far is that from here?"

From the back seat, Sato rang in, "It's 10.2 miles and about eighteen minutes without traffic."

George looked over at his back seat mate who was staring at her phone, then he said, "Well, since we are driving awhile, I guess we can discuss things. Such as, JP, do you think I can get that Cuban sandwich again for dinner?"

Gonzalez's boss abruptly turned around and glared at his junior partner. "Since we are in route, JP, please tell us what you know of the other two incidents."

"Sure, but first, George, I'm sorry. The Cuban sandwich is only at Friday lunch. Tonight, the RC has fried chicken, but nothing like any you have ever had, I guarantee you"

Williams looked at the driver and held his right hand out, making a rolling motion, indicating he wanted to move on to business. Getting the message, JP started the entire rundown.

"Thursday was a really beautiful day for March, like mid 80s and sunny. So, I had just walked out of the Annex to scope out the area by the pier. When I got close, I heard screaming that sounded like kids or maybe teens, so, I ran towards it.

"When I got there, Carol was bent over and throwing up awful green colored stuff and there were four other early 20s types rubbing their arms fiercely. One girl was screaming like wild. I saw Carol hit the sand in her own vomit. So, I grabbed one of the boys and shook him and asked, 'What the hell's going on?' All this guy said is, 'It burns,' and then he starts to turn purple.

"By this time, Steve had run up and I did the only thing I could think to do. I yelled for Steve get these boys into the ocean. I picked up Carol and took the screaming girl, Sally Potter, by the hand and headed to the surf. Somehow, Steve got the other three in the ocean. Someone called the ambulance, cause within ten or fifteen minutes, paramedics were there."

Williams asked, "And everyone was taken to the hospital? The one where we are going?"

"Yes, but the others were released this morning I think." JP shook his head and looked down long enough that Martin thought he might need to grab the wheel, but the Jeep stayed right on A1A.

Continuing on, Barnett said, "The doctors figured out it was a topical poison that all five of them had rubbed on."

From the back, Sato wanted more info. "Do they know which poison?"

"Not exactly. They are sending blood tests and skin samples to the Shands' Hospital. We might know next week."

"Maybe I can figure it out," Betty whispered so low that only George heard.

Williams followed up: "I want to hear exactly how this happened from Ms. Blink, and maybe from the rest of those affected. I assume you have their names and contact info."

Barnett said, "Of course, but you will figure out after talking to Carol that you would learn zero from the other kids."

Martin reinforced his insistence to use his authority: "I appreciate your input, but I will see after the first interview. Then I will want to move on to talk to," Williams started looking at his little notebook, "Ron and Don Gordon. What's the story with that incident?"

"You are in luck. Ron and Don are in the same hospital as Carol, but one floor down, I think. And the story there is a bit more straightforward. Yesterday evening the Gordon boys got on a party boat at the south dock because a woman and two hot college girls asked them if they would like a moonlight cruise in the intercoastal.

About ten minutes into the ride while the boys were putting the moves on the coeds at the front of the boat, it blew up."

"And the woman and the two girls?" asks Williams.

"The girls were thrown over the front, and big surprise, the mystery woman was nowhere to be found." JP made a face with his mouth in shape of an O. Smiling, Barnett added, "And the funny part is the wood from the cabin was splintered and shot into Ron's and Don's asses."

Although George and Betty smiled and laughed a bit instinctively, Williams found this not a laughing matter. But Martin refrained from saying anything to correct the junior agents, as the Jeep was just pulling into the hospital parking lot and he wanted to get on with collecting information. The special agent pushed forward with requests about the other witnesses. "Where are the two girls? Do you have their names? How can we interview them?"

JP explained, "I was able to get some details from the girls, but honestly they were both drunk. Luckily, they did not drown. I really think they don't know much other than the same general description that Carol gave me. Plus, once their fathers showed up, both lawyers at the same firm, it became clear to me that any attempt to milk them for more info would be blocked"

Special Agent Martin Williams did not fear lawyers, and made it clear: "If the bureau needs information from the girls, we will get it. Get me their names and contact information."

Deputy Barnett did not like being given an order by anyone, especially someone he didn't work for, but decided to skip the pushback and just said, "Mary has it, if you ever need it. Let's go in and see if we can get your interviews out of the way"

# 7

# Flagler Hospital

Flagler County, Flagler Beach, Flagler College, Flagler Museum, Flagler Hotel, you name it and on the east coast of Florida there is one named after Henry Flagler, the cofounder of Standard Oil from Ohio who traveled to Jacksonville on the advice of a doctor in New York. The climate in the Sunshine State was the best treatment in 1879 for his wife's failing health. Unfortunately, Mary Flagler died in 1981. But Henry fell in love with her nurse and with Florida, leading to things like marriage, building hotels, buying railroads, and generally putting the Flagler name on everything in his reach.

Flagler Hospital is an unexpectedly nice facility for a town of only 14,000 people. You would not conjecture such an excellent medical campus, especially only thirty minutes from the world class Mayo Clinic in Jacksonville and 100 miles from the Shands Hospital at the University of Florida in Gainesville. But the nation's oldest city has many well-funded investors and contributors, thus, a hospital beyond the town's stature. There is something special about St Augustine that the FBI crew pulling up in a door-less yellow Jeep could not take time to focus on.

As everyone hit the ground, JP went straight to the rear and took two biscuits out of his shorts as he instructed: "Rester." Then heading for the front door with FBI right behind, he said, "I will take you guys to see Carol first. But I have to warn you, this interview must be done very gingerly."

Williams didn't like being warned by this local yokel, but deciding discretion was best. Finding a meaningful clue after the morning's embarrassment was Martin's overriding thought.

As they entered the lobby, JP went straight past the greeting desk without a word and headed to an elevator that was just opening. Two young guys with tattoos and metal bits in strange places stepped out and rushed by. Barnett stepped in and turned around and pressed "5." Gonzalez, the last in, barely missed the door as it closed quickly.

Having already come to visit twice, JP knew exactly where to go. Marching past the nurse's station, Barnett waved to the two female nurses and one male nurse who seemed uninvolved in any pressing activity. Room 515 was a very standard plain hospital affair with light colored walls, a white ceiling and a couple of tan plastic chairs: one roll around backless chair with a red top sat next to the bed. None of this could Carol Blink notice, as she was quite blind.

Each of the agents could not help but notice how attractive and yet innocent the young blonde woman lying in the bed appeared. She evoked the same feeling as when you see a fawn laying in the woods who has been bitten by a snake. You are compelled to help, but how? For some reason she did not yet understand, Betty Sato was very moved emotionally.

JP softly said, "Carol?"

The patient responded, "JP!! I am so glad you are here. You know it's hard for me to tell what time it is. Is it night now?"

"No, beautiful. It's just almost two in the afternoon. I have some friends here that are helping me. Martin, George, and Betty. Can they ask you a few questions about the lady that gave you the 'samples' of suntan oil to use and pass out to your friends? Just in case I missed something."

"Sure," said Carol.

JP wanted to make this as easy as possible: "George is a really cute Cuban guy, would it be ok if he held your hand while he asks a few questions?"

Agent Gonzalez turned to his partners and mouthed silently, *What should I do?*

Carol purred, "I would like that." Then she added "And JP, the doctor said they might take me to the Mayo tomorrow, or is it Monday? Plus, get this! I heard two doctors saying they might fix me with a Jordi Visor."

Already in the process of manually moving George's hand towards Carol's, JP saw two orderlies walking by, with one pushing a cart. Deputy Barnett's expression changed as did the color of his face. Luckily Carol could not see that, as it would have scared her.
   Agents Williams and Sato noticed this, but the third agent was facing the witness as he took her hand.

Barnett tried not to change his tone of voice as he said, "Carol, I need to step out a minute. George will ask you a few questions. But if you don't remember, it is OK. Just say so."

"OK, JP. Come back before you leave."

"Of course. I would never leave without saying goodbye," assures the deputy.

JP turned and bolted towards the door. Williams signaled with his head for Sato to follow, which she gladly did. Betty was not looking forward to watching the interview of this young girl.

"Hey guys," JP yelled as he approached the two orderlies. "I have an important question for you fellows." Betty could not imagine what was going on as the two somewhat awkward mid-twenties men turned to face their unexpected inquisitor.

The taller and less studious looking responded, "Yes, sir, how can we help you?" The shorter not only stayed silent but sheepishly cast his eyes down, clearly uncomfortable with speaking to anyone that carried an aura of authority.

"Kirk or Picard?" asked JP.

Now visibly more engaged, the guys in scrubs looked at each other and then back at JP. "Picard, of course!" in unison.

The deputy responded, "As I guessed, and being in the medical field I wanted to know how you felt about Dr. Crusher making jokes about Worf being paralyzed by a spinal trauma?"

Now the shorter geek was uninhibited, and spoke up with a tone that showed he was offended: "She never did that! That's crazy! Beverly Crusher would ever make fun of any patient, much less a member of the crew."

His more thoughtful and quick-thinking companion butted in before his friend could continue his rant, asking, "This is about the girl in 515? About the visor?"

Betty was not up to speed on what was happening, but she was holding her oversized phone and typing like mad. One might think she was researching *Star Trek* or something of the sort, but that would be very wrong. Sato had much more important questions on her mind.

JP resisted his urge to get super aggressive and went for the mild sauce. "This is about two guys that think they are geniuses **who are actually idiots.** This is about having more empathy with fictional characters than real people. This is about how can you two bozos can ever make up for the damage you may have done. Postulate that hypothesis!"

The shorter was almost shaking, but his friend could get out, "We thought she was asleep. Her eyes were closed."

Deputy JP Barnett was not going for that. "**Listen Einstein**, ever think you might not hold your eyes open if you couldn't, see?"

Before he could blow up, the deputy turned his back and headed back to 515. Betty continued to type, then followed a bit later than usual. The thought ran through the female agent's mind: *Was Mr. Laid Back about to lose his cool with those guys?* As Sato followed JP into the room, George was still holding Carol's hand, and she seemed to be describing her favorite food, which was Mac n' Cheese from Frenchie on Tuesdays.

Sato figured the serious part of the interview was over. Moving in close to where George was, she said to the

blond girl, "I am Betty Sato, and I am here to help you."
As she gently replaced George's hand with hers, Betty
bent over and kissed the patient on the forehead.

JP and both male agents found this display of emotion
by the normally demure Sato as unusual to say the least.
Betty leaned over and whispered in the blind girl's ear.

Williams started to demand a report of what went on in
the hall. In addition, Martin's mind was racing with the
overpowering thought: *What the hell has gotten into
Sato?*

As Betty released her hand and moved away, JP put his
hand on the girl's arm. "Carol, I will be back to see you
soon. And Gidget sends her love and wants me to bring
her over."

Carol smiled and said, "Thanks JP, I would love that!
Gidget is the best, next to you of course."

The FBI agents withdrew and slowly deputy Barnett
backed out the door while keeping an eye on his newly
blind friend. Once in the hall, JP headed towards the exit
sign at the end of the hall, calling out, "Come on, let's get
this over with. The Gordon boys are just one floor down,
we can take the stairs." Moving quicker than normal by a
lot, the agents picked up the pace to follow Barnett down
the stairs.

It saved a lot of time knowing that room 404 would be
right there when opening the stairway door. JP was
ready to get this hospital thing over with. The deputy
headed straight across the hall and into the double
bedroom, instantly calming down and starting to smile as
he saw the patients.

Even Williams was lightened up a bit by the sight, two big burly guys laying each face down in separate beds, each with covers only up to their knees, each with several small bandages on their upper legs and lower back, and each with large white bandages taped on each cheek of their butts.

Sato covered her mouth and hoped no one heard the giggles. But they did.

JP said, "Hey! Don and Ron, I have three FBI agents with me, and they wanted to know about the woman that invited you on the party boat."

*Don:* "Really? Cool, the FBI, cool."
*Ron:* "Awesome, do they have badges? I want to see one."
*Don:* "Me too, do we get to see a lineup?"
*Ron:* "I hope so, I can describe her. She was 32B."
*Don:* "No she wasn't, she was at least 34C."
*Ron:* "No way, dude. Clearly that's crap, 32B."
*Don:* "Well she had a skinny little tight ass."
*Ron:* "That's bullshit, she had a plump bubble butt."
*Don:* "I'll take either," laughing like a fool.
*Ron:* "Ditto, dude," with matching foolish sounds.
*Don:* "She was a dirty blonde."
*Ron:* "Bet she was dirty, but dude, she's a red head."
*Don:* "Really? Hot! I wonder if the carpet matches the drapes?"
*Ron:* "Yea, that's great when the carpet matches the drapes!"
*Don:* "I bet the carpet needs to be vacuumed."

By now these idiots were laughing like hyaenas. And Betty Sato could not help to think: *First two smart guys make a big mistake due to a woman with her eyes closed, then two buffoons count on mistakes that women make with their eyes wide open. The irony is so thick that you could not cut through it with the Enterprise's entire phaser bank.*

"SHUT THE HELL UP!" yelled Williams, clearly losing his patience.

Just in time, a tall stocky guy with tan cowboy hat, red western shirt, pressed and pleated jeans and a cigar in his mouth walked in holding two ice cream cones.

JP said, "Jack, I am glad you are here," in a clear attempt to get things back on track. "These FBI agents would like to talk to your boys."


As the man walked in front of the boys and handed each an ice cream, he pulled the cigar from his mouth, turned to the agents and said, "I'm Jack Gordon. I am the biggest used car dealer on the first coast, with lots in Jax , Saint Augustine  and opening soon in Daytona. I hope you Feds are here to look into JP's pal Steve attacking my sons!"

*JP:* "Jack, we settled this back in August."
*Jack:* "The hell we did. My boys maybe would have been first string guards with the Gators, except Steve attacked them."
*JP:* "Well, they should not have been trying to grope Songbird Wilson."
*Jack*: "You didn't see that."
*JP:* "Five other people did."
*Jack:* "Steve didn't have break their arms. I don't care if he is some sort of war hero."
*JP:* "Well, Don and Ron should know better than for each of em to take a swing at him."
*Jack:* "You should have still arrested him. It's assault."

*JP:* "Jack, Jack, please calm down. We went over this. If I took this incident to the DA, he would have charged your boys with sexual assault on a minor. That's serious business. We are lucky Gidget was willing to let it slide with an apology."

*Jack:* "I know, JP. I am just so disappointed. This was their year to be on the Gators. Even if they were second string, it would have been fantastic. I think about it all the time."

*JP:* "Jack, still Jameson?"

*Jack:* "Yep."

*JP:* "How many on the way to get ice cream?"

*Jack:* "A couple."

*JP:* "Couple, like two?"

*Jack:* "Maybe four."

*JP:* "Stay here with your boys at least a couple hours before going back to work."

*Jack:* "I was going to stay till dinner time."

*JP:* "Good. I will have a nurse get you some coffee, still black with couple of sugars, no cream?"

*Jack:* "Thanks JP. Sorry for the rant."

*JP:* "No problem, buddy. Do me a favor. This is Agent Williams, Agent Gonzales, and Agent Sato. Can you get the boys to be serious about answering their questions?"

*Jack:* "If you want me to, I will see to it. The boys will answer anything, or I'll kick their asses."

*What a vexing conundrum,* thought Williams, the seasoned special agent. *Law enforcement that ignores sexual assault on a minor then uses it to maintain order and later receive cooperation.* Which was much more complex analysis than his right-hand man, George, who just thought, *So cool that JP gets along with this guy so well.* No such attention to the matter was present for the tiny female agent, who was madly typing on her huge phone.

"Coffee coming up," was yelled back from the self-appointed food runner as JP exited the room tailed by his shadow from the last excursion into the halls. Dr. Isaac Cohen, chief of medicine, was just leaving the 4th floor nurses' station when he saw Barnett and Sato headed his way.

"JP, how are you doing?" yelled the doctor.

"I'm fine, Doc, how are you? This is agent Betty Sato with the FBI. I am so glad I ran into you. I wanted to ask about Carol Blink. What do you know about her condition, or have you found out what the poison was?"

Doctor Cohen responded, "I'm great, thanks. As for Carol, we do not know yet. It is unclear if it's still affecting her optic nerves or if it can be reversed or if it's permanent damage. We are thinking the poison is thallium, which is fairly easy to get."

Not a part of the conversation except as an observer, Betty uncharacteristically interjected, "I do not think so. You would see nausea and vomiting, but the neuropathies would not normally be optic."

Shocked, the doctor turned to the almost child-sized woman. "Well, we have sent samples to Shands in Gainesville and we will know maybe tomorrow, but certainly by Monday. I still think it is likely thallium."

JP was taken aback as Betty proceeded, "Monday will be too late to find out! Have you considered a venom?"

The Chief of Medicine is starting to wonder what an FBI agent could know about this and corrected her: "Young lady, this is not a snake bite."

Tempted to list all the options and probabilities, Betty decided to just state the summary: "There are more venomous fish than venomous snakes."

Sensing this was headed in the wrong direction, JP placed his hand on the doctor's arm, saying, "How are Laura and the kids? Did Ethan pick a medical school yet?"

Isaac was glad to discuss his family. "Oh yes! He got into Mount Sinai. We are very happy and soon to be broke." Doctor Dad laughed and added,"He is going to specialize in radiology."

Sato blurted out, "That's a mistake! AI will make obsolete human analysis of images before he can get out. In fact, it already has, and it's only vested interests and inertia that continues the current backward use of humans to 'read' (as she added air quotes) digital images."

Dr. Cohen was not amused, and struck back, "Well, maybe I should suggest Ethan switch to plastic surgery. Lots of money, and there is an endless supply of women who need boob jobs," as he stares very obviously at Betty's chest.

Not fazed by this, Sato was about to point out that with the early detection accomplished by big data analysis and proper AI it could mean many people would be alive day, possibly even her mother. But thankfully from JP's point of view, a very frustrated Special Agent rushed into the group and declared, "Those Gordon boys are idiots!!" before Betty could continue.

"Dr. Cohen, this is agent Williams and…" JP turned back, where he expected George. Instead, way back at the entrance to room 404, Jack is standing close to

George, and they are shaking hands. The Latino Fed had his other hand resting on the car dealer's shoulder. The surprise and happiness and hopefulness of this sight brightened JP's mood.

Ignoring the need for normal social greeting, Martin continued, "How can two grown men not remember whether a woman that they just saw last night was blond, brunette, or red headed, tall or short, straight or curly hair, pants or a dress, or even agree on one single detail? I just do not get it."

Still feeling feisty, Betty Sato answered, "**I do**. They do not actually see women, except as toys. And they were focused on how to use two coeds who they felt entitled to. Maybe they are not idiots, just predators who could not be distracted from their prey."

The three men looked at each other with a collective fear of commenting on this analysis.
After a long moment of dead air, JP looked at the chief of medicine and asked, "Can you get a nurse or orderly to take a cup of coffee to Jack?"

The doctor, happy to back out of this mess, volunteered, "I'll do it myself. I want to talk to him about when we can release his sons."

"Thanks. Two sugars, no cream, if you can," added Barnett.

Dr. Cohen was just departing, as George rejoined the group and asked, "What did I miss?"

Williams responded, "Nothing important." Still frustrated, he added, "Since we are in Saint Augustine, let's look for a hotel." As he headed for the exit.

The doors to the elevator opened and there was a young black nurse pushing an old white woman in a wheelchair. Williams charged in, even though normally he might wait for the next car. The others followed in and the fit was a bit tight.

The nurse said to the woman she was transporting, "Once we get you in your son's car, will you remember to go by Publix to pick up the medicine the doctor called in? It's important you start it tomorrow morning."

The patient being wheeled out replied, "Can you tell my son? And tell him to get me some apple pie? Publix has great apple pie."

The nurse smiles, "Yes they do. I will tell your son that the doctor prescribed apple pie."

The old woman and her escort both laughed, as the elevator door opened on the ground floor.

# 8

# Back to Crescent Beach

After the crew politely slow walked out behind the elderly woman being pushed to patient pickup in a wheelchair, they picked up the pace to the Wrangler. JP said, "Give me a minute with the dogs." Going straight to the tailgate, he opened and pointed at the lawn to the side of the hospital - "être occupé." Sel and Poivre jumped out and headed straight for the grass. Each circled around a tight area, sniffing as they went, did their business, and returned to the back of the rear of the Jeep.

Sato had to inquire "JP, do your dogs only respond to French?" To which she quickly informed "No, they know English and some Spanish, they just prefer French". Betty was unsure if this was another joke.

With everyone in their assigned seats, the yellow doorless topless wonder fired back up as the driver said: "Martin, I have an important matter to discuss with you."

"Really, what could that be?" The backseat passengers perked up their eyes, even if it meant one had to stop looking and entering data in an oversized screen.

"The good people of Crescent Beach rely on me to guard and defend their interests."

"I am glad you see it that way, but there are also higher standards too," said Williams.

The deputy knew this was not going his way, but needed to keep the thought flowing, as he added, "Maybe, but not in this regard. Our citizens have been sending tax dollars to Washington, DC since at least 1914."

As they sped towards A1A, all agents are thinking, *What the hell is JP talking about?*

Barnett continued, "And you come here on a mission to supposedly help us out. And I thank you for your effort. But I am not sure your heart is in the right place, and it's my job to call you out on it."

Special Agent Williams was about fed up. "If you do not like the way I am running our investigation, you can just get out of the way!"

JP was actually happy with that response, as it's what he expected, so he was ready with, "I am not going to do that, to protect both you and my town. So here is the deal. You mentioned finding a room in Saint Augustine. I object to that."

"What? Do you want us to sleep on the beach? Or stay at your place to save tax dollars?"

"Well, I have slept on the beach before. It's very relaxing. But no, I am suggesting that after Crescent Beach has sent you all that tax money, you could at least spend some of it with **us**."

Sato and her constant web search were way ahead of Williams, and she showed it by saying, "The Seahorse Inn, built in 1952, renovated in 1981, expanded in 2000, and just updated in 2016. 32 rooms with full AC, cable TV, wi-fi, view of the ocean, and breakfast included for all guests, according to Yelp."

The driver was delighted to have what he saw as support from the back seat, adding "Plus the owner, Alice Allen, is super nice, and keeps a very clean place."

Martin found this a long way around the barn and said so. "This was all about getting us to stay in Crescent Beach? Why didn't you just say so to start with?"

"Because, if I didn't kill some time, you would insist on discussing the case. And I prefer to enjoy the ride. See, we are getting close already, and soon you will see the ocean on the left."

Martin tried to enjoy the distraction a bit. "I've seen the ocean, but maybe you are right that it would not hurt to see it again. Actually, I was hoping to see that old Spanish fort in Saint Augustine. Maybe I can catch it later."

Sato struck again: "Castillo de San Marcos, constructed from 1672 until 1695, the oldest masonry fort in the continental United States. Made of coquina to be impenetrable to enemy attack and fire resistant. The fort came under fire by the British forces in 1702, 1728, and 1740. However, the British were never able to take the city of St. Augustine by force due to it being guarded by this fort. Castillo de San Marcos was recognized as a National Monument in 1924."

Martin responded, "Gee thanks, Betty, I guess I can skip the tour now. Maybe I can settle for seeing a bit of the Atlantic."

JP said, "Exactly, and if you get a second-floor room at the Seashore, you can see the sun come up over it tomorrow morning. Double plus plus! And it's walking distance to the Annex and the RC. That's a super plus in case your guys drink too much at dinner."

"We are not drinking at dinner!" insisted the lead FBI agent.

Barnett raised his voice just an octave. "Agent Williams, you will not have a nice red wine with the best dinner you have had all year? I am amazed! I know you are a bit, let us say 'serious,' since 'anal' is not that pleasant a term, but I never thought you were some kind of uncivilized cretin that could not even enjoy a good Malbec or Cab with dinner." Then JP smiled and looked at the guy to his right instead of the road.

By now George was laughing too hard to be appropriate, as he did not have the cultural advantage of silently giggling into a hand over the mouth as Betty was doing.

"OK, actually, I would enjoy wine with dinner," said Martin as he lightened up a bit. "Of course, in New Orleans we never consider wine as real drinking. But I have a serious question for you, Mr. Smart Ass. Why would I drink a Malbec or Cab, if there was a nice Bordeaux available?" At last, there was a smile from the special agent.

"I can assure you, Frenchie has some excellent Boudreaux on hand. I will see to it that you get a bottle."

'
"A glass, maybe two if it's truly excellent." Actually, he was not thinking about it, but Williams had already smiled more today than in the last week. Frustrated, sure, but a little entertainment was not that normal in Martin's life, so, this felt OK.

Rolling down the coastal highway, there was plenty of ocean to see to the east, but Williams was looking in all directions, as always. One must be aware of their surroundings. Martin's training was always in play. To the west a large green sign got his attention. "Frank Butler Park, where have I heard of that name before?"

Feeling the agent's eyes upon him and thinking a response might be needed, JP looked over. "Maybe from your family or someone you knew who vacationed there."

Of course, there was someone sitting in the back seat who held the clue in her hand. Betty had to speak loudly as the wind in the Jeep at 55mph is a bit noisy: "Frank B. Butler was an African American entrepreneur in Saint Augustine in the early 1900s. He owned several businesses and started buying land on Anastasia Island in 1927. After World War II, Butler developed the property to a resort area for African Americans. Later, Mr. Butler sold part of the property to the State of Florida for development of a state park for blacks."

This information left all the sleuths silent for long enough that they approached their destination. But thoughts were ignited.

JP and Martin did not know it, but they were thinking exactly the same thing: *How sad and disappointing that we used to need to have separate beaches and parks.*

George could not help but remember his grandfather again, for the fourth time today! "The most beautiful beaches on earth are in Cuba, George. I hope when the gangster communists are overthrown, you will get to go and see them. Maybe even you can move our family back. Cuba is truly the most beautiful place on earth. The mountains, the beaches, the fertile land, the music, the food, the people. I hate Fidel and hope he burns in hell."

Betty had not really paid a lot of attention to the history she conveyed, until after she finished. That is when she started to think about it and recall the stories of the Japanese in the USA right after World War II. Sato wondered, at that time, would any Japanese be welcome on any beach or in any park, anywhere in America?

A few Minutes later, with the Atlantic clearly visible to the east of A1A, in a spot with no building on the east side, there was the Seahorse Inn on the west of that same road. Symmetrical, with a wide entrance in the middle, flanked by two 8-foot-tall white concrete seahorses on 2-foot-tall pedestals, the top of the head of each statue as tall as the hotel's first floor. The second floor had a porch that ran the entire length of the building. Doors on both floors faced out towards the ocean and had gold plated numbers attached at eye level.

Renovated or not, this was clearly not the class of hotel that Williams was used to being treated to on the people's dime. But Martin was not in the mood to fight the importance of local businesses. Plus, the replacement specialty team would be in by Monday, so it was only three nights. As JP parked in front he said, "It's just past four, so I am sure you can check right in. I guess check-in time is three."

Williams thought, *Who the hell does he think he is kidding? There're only three other cars here, and probably at least one belongs to the staff.*

The deputy and Williams walked in to secure the rooms, and sure enough Alice was at the front desk. She was glad to see JP, and even more happy to get three unexpected rooms rented for three nights! When it's off season, you take what you can get. The agents got the nicest rooms on the second floor, with great views of the beach.

George and Betty stayed outside, the latter sitting and typing on her phone, the former getting out to stretch his legs and trying to see if he could make friends with the two dogs that he had insulted only seven hours before. When JP exited between the statues, he was delighted to see Sel and Poivre being petted on the head. Barnett walked up and acted as if he could secretly hand two biscuits to Agent Gonzalez. The Barbets did not mind that snacks were originally from their master, and not from their new friend. Each took their treat from the Latino's outstretched hand.

The senior FBI member approached, with three sets of keys hanging from his large right hand. The deputy announced, "Let's get dinner early. If you guys go get your car and bring your luggage back, I can go by my office, answer a few emails, stop by my house and change into evening wear." JP, of course, was joking about that last statement.

Sato responded, "Do we need something dressier? I only packed work clothes, and one exercise outfit."

JP looked slowly up and down at what appeared to be three adults dressed like people going to a costume party as penguins. "No, you guys will be fine. Do you want to ride to your Kia or walk?" He said, smiling in a playful manner. "I can pick you up at 5:30."

Williams said, "It's across the street and two blocks down. We will walk."

As the FBI agents watched the Jeep pull out for the couple of blocks' trip to the Annex, the team leader started walking the short trek and observed, "Deputy Jean Pierre Barnett is way too relaxed and laid back for my taste. I am not sure he is up to the task. I have never found these southern good-ole boy types very impressive. Tomorrow we might need to work more independently of JP." Then Williams stopped before he could add what he was thinking: *This stupid jerk is racist cracker, who probably needs to be arrested himself.*

Sato volunteered, "I have an idea on tracking the explosive used on the boat," feeling she needed to make up for the snafu on the original lead. And since she did not hear the encouragement she expected, she added, "On the deputy, I do not have enough data to draw a final conclusion."

George chimed in, "I think JP is cool as hell," and then in response to the two glares he received, he qualified, "I mean, JP seems to know the civilians well, gets along with them, and has the support of all the locals." Williams let that go as they got in the tiny red rent-a-box on wheels and returned to the Seahorse Inn.

# 9

# Origin of the Barbets

Although JP was, in his mind, not really late, some people view ten minutes one way or the other as a big deal. Which explained why only one of the three in penguin disguise was beyond just a bit impatient. The other two agents were not as concerned with the deputy being punctual as they were with their boss's growing irritation with the assignment. As the Jeep pulled up in front of the giant seahorses, Williams yelled, "I thought you said 5:30? We have been waiting."

"Hmmm, I thought it was 5:30," said JP, looking at his left wrist where a watch might be, if Barnett owned a watch. The deputy signaled with his right hand to get in, and JP continued, "I hope you guys are hungry. I know that fried chicken sounds boring, but just wait."

Sato, as she took her seat behind the driver, commented, "I do not really eat fried food. Maybe there will be something a little lighter."

George said, "I must say, my mother's fried chicken was never that good, but there is a place in Little Havana that had the best fried chicken, somehow they seasoned and fried a complete chicken to perfection. It was just fabulous. I forgot the name of the place, but it was on 12th street, I am fairly sure, anyway."

Serious as ever, Williams pointed out, "I am certain dinner will be fine and we will all be well fed. There is business at hand. JP, Agent Sato believes the boat was blown up with Tannerite. Do you know anyone in

Crescent Beach that would be keeping Tannerite? Or any place that might be selling it?"

Deputy Barnett did his thoughtful petting goatee thing and said, "Hmmm, anyone could have it, but I've never heard of anyone here using it. I guess maybe to blow up a stump. No stores that I know of sell it. You would have to go to Saint Augustine or Daytona probably to get some. But wait, that makes no sense. Don't you have to mix it and then hit it with a high-powered rifle shot to get it to go off?"

Williams concurred, "That's what I understand. But Betty has a different theory of how to use fireworks and a timer."

JP nodded his head as the Wrangler pulls into the front of the RC. Luckily there was one parking place left. "Well, that's an interesting theory."

George observed, "Wow, it seems much busier than lunch."

"It's never too early to start the weekend," threw out the local, jumping out and heading for the back to release his constant companions. And, of course, JP was right. Friday is a great day to take off early and see what fun can be had before Monday rolls back around.
Quickly moving up the steps and holding the door and bowing with one arm swung out to welcome his guests, Barnett smiled as the tall agent bringing up the rear almost hit his head on that somewhat low hanging sign.

Darker and nosier than he remembered from just six hours ago, Williams thought it seemed like a different place completely. There was a chair placed on a four-foot-tall box at the end of the bar. The agent looked around to take in details as he had been trained to do. The picture of Elvis had been replaced with a poster of Lou Reed (although Martin could not ID the ex-Velvet Underground front man) and President Kennedy's picture had been replaced with a poster of Richard Nixon (which Williams could easily recognize but could not support. What agent could? Considering how 'Tricky Dick' had tried to subvert the FBI and turn it into his own private political arm. Many at the bureau, including Martin, felt no love for Nixon or his party).

Noting that the entire feel of the RC had changed, including "Bohemian Rhapsody" in the background instead of the Everly Brothers, Martin saw one thing was the same, as the white & black dogs rushed to lie under the pool table.

The group arrived at the same table where they'd had lunch to find a bottle with a black and gold label marked 2007 Chateau Palmer Margaux sitting in the middle. There was a folded note under the bottle. JP picked up the bottle and handed it to Williams, then he took the card, read it and slipped it in his back pocket.

Williams inspected the bottle closely and turned to deputy Barnett. "This is too much. I cannot accept this."

JP grinned and said, "Damn straight you can't, it's for all of us!"

"I do not need to drink," Sato volunteered, as she knew only a small amount of alcohol had a large impact on her judgement. Something she found out in college, which could have led to an unwanted sexual encounter had it not been for her mother insisting her daughters take those lessons from Master Ito five days a week for years. Instincts and reflexes can be learned and reinforced until they kick in without thought. That's the point of constant training. Which explained how a certain male student with yellow fever who decided to act on his desires found himself on the floor with a broken wrist.

JP quickly agreed Betty could skip the Bordeaux. "Great, more for the rest of us," to which George and even Martin laughed.

A woman with short black spiky hair, wearing a black spaghetti strap top with clearly no bra and super tight black leather pants that hugged her ankles about one inch above black pointed-toe mini boots appeared behind JP. He quickly turned around, perhaps because she grabbed his butt. "Joan! You surprised me - thanks for having Frenchie pick us out a Bordeaux."

Quickly turning to the group JP said, "Let me introduce Joan Jett, the proprietor of this joint." Barnett stroked his goatee and slipped a finger over his lips, then started what seemed to the agents to be a very odd re-introduction. "Joan, these are agents from the FBI who are here to help with our problem." As he introduced them.

Joan moved close to Betty and started to run her hand over her the agent without touching her hair, shoulders, and arms. "Ohhh, Agent Sato, yes, very intriguing," Ms. Jett said in a tone that made this female agent very uncomfortable.

This situation was even making Williams a bit uneasy. So, in order to move towards a more comfortable and understandable discussion, Martin said, "JP, everything seems a bit different here than I expected, except your dogs are under the pool table. That must be where they think they belong."

Agent Williams didn't really know what a dog might think. His mother never allowed him to have one. They scared her. In fact, his mother did not like any pets, although he got to have a turtle when he was five, but only after several months of begging. Like probably millions of kids before and after him, he named his turtle "Myrtle."

Joan interjected her take on where Sel and Poivre were: "Of course they belong there, as that's how JP got them," turning her attention to the group as if to recount the entire sordid story.

Instantly JP insisted, "The FBI is not interested in that, Joan."

Williams responded, "Actually the agency might be very interested in that."

The proprietor continued, "Oh, I guess all I should say is, if you are a smart ass from Quebec stopping on your way to Lauderdale, don't bet all your vacation money and prized puppies on being able to beat a local goofball in pool."

Deputy Barnett did not really want to go into some long discussion about whether gambling was legal or immoral. Especially since his attitude was that it's hard to lose your life savings at a pool or card table compared to the perfectly legal crap on Wall Street. JP demanded, "Joan, these important agents do not have time for such trivial matters. They need to eat and we need glasses with a corkscrew."

Joan replied, "Yes sir," with a tone of sarcasm, and pointed to the bartender while waving a hand in the air in a circular motion. "I will go get your dinners myself." She turned to Sato and blew an air kiss. Soon thereafter four glasses were brought over by a friendly-looking but silent older woman who opened the wine and walked away.

As soon as Joan departed, Williams turned to JP and asked, "OK, so what's the deal? The owner changes her hair and clothes and name from lunch to dinner. Does that happen every day, and what's the deal with the role playing? Clearly her name is not Donna Reed or Joan Jett. Who is she really? Why the charade?"

JP fell back on stroking the goatee while thinking, or at least appearing to be thinking. "Well. That's a lot of questions, and I am certain none of the answers lead to anything which requires investigation by the FBI. But just let me say, the RC closes at two after lunch, and Donna takes a rest, and when it reopens at five, Joan is ready to make all the customers happy."

"That's not an answer," Martin pointed out.

"Some mysteries are left unsolved. For example, how does Frenchie get the fried chicken on Friday nights to be so damn good? And how does he make broccoli that even I will eat? And what's in the rice that makes it plain and light even though it's super flavorful? And who gets the extra wine that Betty is turning down?"

George said, "I am ready to find out."

As Williams started to press further, he was cut off by light clapping from the bar and a few tables. "Must be Darryl," JP guessed without turning around. Of course, sure enough a young tall slender black kid had just walked through the front door carrying a guitar in one hand and a small electric amp in the other. JP turned around and gave the musician a thumbs up, as the amp was plugged in to the wall socket behind the chair which had been set out for Darryl.

Joan walked up carrying a large tray with four plates. As she serviced the sleuths she yelled out, "Darryl, LIGHT MY FIRE, baby!"

Without delay the boy sat down and started what could only be called an amazing cover of The Doors' classic. After a long bluesy intro his baritone voice kicked in, this moving rendition did indeed light everyone's fire.

By the end of the first verse, George Gonzalez was all smiles. "This is fabulous. I love it. The music and the food! What a great place!"

Sato had one piece of broccoli and said, "Very interesting. How is this done? Very different."

"It's caramelized," said Williams, who'd learned plenty about cooking during his first two decades in The Big Easy. Of course, how could anyone spend twenty years in New Orleans and not soak up tons of information concerning gastronomical delights?

Everyone continued to sample each of the three dishes on their plate, except Betty, who did not touch her chicken. About the time that Darryl was transitioning to where the familiar organ solo would have been, which he reimagined in an energic blues guitar style, George said, half kidding, "Sato, if you don't want that chicken, I can take it off your hands."

JP did not want to see that happen, commenting, "Betty, it may look like it's greasy, but it's not. Just try it."

Williams had to second that suggestion: "I have only had chicken like this once, it was in a diner in the Quarter. Crispy outside, moist inside, and not a hint of grease. I am not sure how's it's done. When I went back to get it again, in that little diner, it had changed. They told me the chef had left without giving notice and they could never replicate it."

As the petite woman took her first bite, she smiled in disbelief and took another and another, much to Gonzalez's disappointment, as it was clear he would not be getting a second round from Sato's plate. Darryl was coming to the big finish, which certainly drew Martin's attention, as did the double shot of Jack that the barmaid looked to be pouring in reach of the kid. Sensing what was coming, Williams took a sip of wine, got up, and headed towards the end of the bar.

Maybe it was because Darryl was so good, maybe it was because he was black, maybe it was because he looked so young, but it was unlikely it was because the special agent wanted a shot of Jack too. Martin hurried to the bar, appearing in the only way he knew how, authoritative and somewhat threatening. "**How old are you?**" is ALL Darryl heard over the clapping. Which was too bad because what was actually said was, "I wanted to tell you that was the best cover I have heard. But I would like to ask: how old are you?"

As the special agent looked down and noticed small round scars on the back of the musician's hands, a few up his arm, and one on the left side of his neck, he continued,
"Listen, son…"

Daryll promptly interrupted, "**I'm not your son!**"

Martin wanted to offer good vibes to the kid, that he could see had likely had a hard life so far: "Sorry. I am just trying to help."

"**Bullshit**. Where were you to help when I rode into town with nothing but a bike and a guitar? Where were you when I be hungry and needin to crash? How about when my old man showed up? Did you kick his ass and tell him he would be in jail or worse if he ever came back?"

The barmaid handed Darryl another shot and said, "Roll on, baby," as the shot disappeared. Williams stood still, not knowing the next best move, but the musician did roll on. "Grandpa, did you get me a place to live? Into school? A tutor? A job? Hell no, and you have the balls…"

Then, stopping mid-sentence, Darryl felt the familiar hand of Barnett on his arm. The musician heard JP say, "I see you boys are getting along just great. I just wanted to stop by and say I have to step out for about thirty minutes, just long enough for Martin to get a fabulous dessert. Darryl, you should drop back in the kitchen, Frenchie has something special for you."

Much to Williams' surprise, the boy stood up and hugged JP. As Darryl walked towards the kitchen, he yelled back, "There be some Motown later for those OLD enough to remember."

Sato appeared in the corner of JP's eye, as the deputy gave Martin a hint: "Between the lemon and raspberry tart, take the raspberry. No wait, you can have mine, so try both."
    Betty added, "You can give mine to George." Then Sato followed the deputy to the door.

# 10

## The Beach at night

Once outside on the porch of the RC, Deputy Barnett turned to Sato and steps up toe to toe, as his constant companions slipped out the door.

*What he is doing? Is he going to attack me or try to kiss me?* Betty's thought as she looked straight up due to the height differential.

"Just where do you think you are going, young lady?" demands JP.

Sato is thinking *What a brazen question. I am a grown woman, an FBI agent. Where does he get off with the attitude?* However, Betty's response was much more accommodating. "I just thought that so far it's been way more interesting to follow you." Then she lowered her eyes some, reached down to pet Sel and implored, "Could I go with you, or is your task too private?"

Stepping back and returning to the old habit of playing with the goatee while thinking, Barnett said, "OK, but it's nothing really exciting. And we should be back real soon anyway." The automatic pathway lights came on as they walked down the steps, the sunset that triggers them being much earlier in March than most of the year. "It's only a few blocks, so we can walk, unless you find it too chilly."

Betty smiled. "Right, as if 70 degrees is chilly."

"Actually, I think it's probably down to 65," said JP while wrapping his arms around himself and making a *brr* sound. "But no kidding, I saw on my phone that it could get down to 45 tomorrow night."

"That's still not too cold. By the way, what are we doing?" asked Sato.

"Maybe not cold to you, but I may have to wear pants all weekend. I sure hope not. And we are not doing much. There is someone living with me. I promised to check in on them before dark."

Sato felt her heart sink a little, but she didn't know exactly why. Changing the topic as Betty pulls her massive phone from her jacket pocket, she said, "You said you saw the weather on your phone. I hardly ever see you take it out. Even George looks at his a few times an hour. Don't you need it for business?"

"It vibrates when it wants my attention. Don't your toys do that?" joked JP.

As Betty struggled to interpret that and think of how to respond, they arrived at JP's house. There stood waiting a very tall guy with short blonde hair which was stylishly spiked.

"You   are   late." Most people in Crescent Beach speak in 3/4 time (with one notable fast speaking exception). But as Steve continued it was clear he was communicating in 3/4s of 3/4 time, which might be 9/16 time. But needless to say, MUCH slower than most anyone talks. "You   are   late,   JP," Steve repeated.

As Sato sized up this guy, late 20s / early 30s, surfer-type look, flip flops, a very noticeable scar on the right side of his neck that appeared to extend under his t-shirt (which had a cat on a surfboard printed on the front, with the words under the image **'Be a Cool Cat in Crescent Beach'**). Below Steve's yellow and blue board shorts there was a large white bandage taped to his right thigh.

Barnett was avoiding the topic of tardiness completely. "Steve, you changed your hair. It looks great."

"Gidget did it. She said it was a reward," as the slow talker looked towards Betty.

JP responded, "It looks great, really. Steve, this is a friend of mine who is visiting town. Her name is Betty."

"Friend? Like girlfriend? JP has a girlfriend?" he said in a playful a way, which made Steve seem much younger than he was, like elementary school age.

Betty instantly interjected, "We are just professional friends," as JP stepped past Steve to open the front door.

"Steve, do you need anything to eat before going to bed?" asked Barnett.

"No, Gidget got me a burger and fries when she did my hair."

As they stepped through the door, Sato was taken aback. A large room with all different sizes of tubes hanging from the ceiling, some metal, some wooden, and two that were glass with walls covered in what appeared to be egg cartons greeted her. There were two reel to reel tape recorders, on tables on opposite walls. The futon on the floor seemed out of place surrounded by bass guitars, a tall set of bongo drums, a small set of traditional drums you might see in a rock band, a saw like one might cut a tree down with, and a bow like you would play a violin with. On the floor not far from the door, a medium-sized brown piece of luggage sat with its top not completely closed, as if someone had been packing and stopped.

The deputy took Steve by the arm and softy said, "I saw JJ today. She said hi."

Steve looked down for a long while, then replied, "Oh, Hi," as he waved in the air as if the salutation could be returned in real time and from far away.

Then, continuing, Steve asked, "It's going to be safe?"

"Yes, I have put rebar in the walls and roof, and your door is steel, only you can open it. Plus, I have a secret system of alarms connected to my phone." JP did not feel bad about repeating the same lies he told every night. He knew it was the best thing he could do.

"Can you and Sel and Poivre play 'Billie Jean' while I fall asleep?"

Deputy Barnett instantly responded, "That's a great idea. We will try and see if we can." Of course, he knew they could, as it was the same request every evening, so, he and the Barbets had it down. Of course, his dogs were not always perfectly in sync.

Steve and JP headed down a small hallway that led towards the 'secure' bedroom.

Sato felt it was best to stay put, which it probably was. Might not have been best to slightly open the top of the luggage, but everyone occasionally surrenders to curiosity. In the case, she found hundreds of pieces of brown paper sheets, each with charcoal drawings. Betty only noticed in detail two. One a beach with a small girl in a tiny bikini holding a rather short surfboard, the other an ocean with a surfer in the distance that looked like they were standing on one hand.

The caregiver appeared and smiled. "I see you found my suitcase of memories." JP went straight to the bongos. Before Betty could start with apologies and dozens of questions, she heard the intro to "Billie Jean" in the air. The Barbets ran to the corner by the saw and grabbed in their mouths two large drumsticks, one each. Custom sticks with a ball on the end made of tightly wrapped leather strips.

After JP started his bongo intro, Sato, her mouth wide open, watched as the dogs ran from tube to tube. Each canine in its own pattern, pounding out the familiar tune which almost everyone knows. Sometimes hitting metal, sometimes wood, sometimes striking low, sometimes jumping high.

JP stopped his drumming and when the amazed woman looked over, he signaled towards the door, then with one hand made a circle in the air that his furry musical friends could see.

Once outside, Sato exclaimed, "That's amazing. How did you train them to do that? Did you build that room like that? Is that where you record the tapes in your car? Did you write that song? It sounds familiar."

JP held up his finger to her lips before any more questions could be thrown out as he thought, *She thinks I wrote "Billie Jean." What planet is this girl from? She does not know about otters, plantains, or Michael Jackson!*

After a bit of silence and a look toward the ocean, he decided to test the 'is she an alien' theory' by checking something Betty should know. JP jumped to the most popular entertainment franchise on earth. Thus, he began the experiment: "To protect the world from devastation! To unite all peoples within our nation!"

Without skipping a beat, the woman who did not know what an otter was, had never heard of a plantain, nor could identify Michael Jackson songs, responded quickly, "To denounce the evils of truth and love. To extend our reach to the stars above."

And looking at each other, they both broke out laughing uncontrollably.

As they regained their composure, JP said, "Speaking of stars above, I always like to stand by the surf and look up right after it gets dark."

Betty wanted to add to her list of questions: *What is this Team Rocket routine about?* But before she could speak, the deputy grabbed her hand and took off across A1A towards the beach. Her choice was, pull back and stay with feet planted, or follow. She took the later.

Once they reached the sand, her hand was released. Stepping on to the firm beach of eastern Florida, Betty was surprised it was like walking on a sidewalk. *This is nothing like California,* she thought without giving any mind to how obviously understated that thought was. Florida vs California: might as well be Earth vs Krypton.

JP strolled right up to the edge of the surf and looked up, characteristically petting his own beard. "What do you see up there?" he said, inquiring into the air.

Looking up in a way Betty had not since 8th grade astronomy class, she said, "Well, I see Mars, of course. I think I can see Mercury. Lots of stars, but I have forgotten the names of many constellations." As Betty reached for her phone, a leathery hand stopped her.

"No cheating," commanded JP.

Since the challenge was put down, Betty responded in kind, "OK, Mr. Star Gazer, what do you see?"

Although accustomed to this night sky, no such familiarity was required for JP's response.
  "I see a woman wearing a metal breastplate and a helmet beset with jewels." The deputy's focus intent on the heavens, Barnett continued, "In her right hand is a diamond-shaped shield, and in her left hand the severed head of a man which she holds by the hair."

"What? There's no constellation like that!" protested Betty.

JP was not ready to give up yet. "And in her other hand there is an axe with a drop of blood dripping from the blade."

"That's three hands!" Sato exclaimed.

"Yes, and in her fourth hand she wields her most mighty weapon, a small portable computer, no wait…... it's actually a giant cellphone."

"So, is that the way you envision me?" asked Betty, placing both hands on her hips.

JP explained, "Oh no, not at all. I envision you in a rather short red plaid pleated skirt, with a white-man-tailored shirt, red plaid tie, white knee-high socks, and black patent leather shoes." Then, pointing at her face, "The glasses are the right color, but they should be big and round like saucers."

Still with the confrontational hands to hip stance, she said, "You have been watching too much anime."

For the second time in one evening, JP turned to Betty and stepped-up toe to toe. Again, she thought, *What he is doing? Is he going attack me or try to kiss me?*

"Take it back this minute, young lady!" demanded the man towering over Betty.

"What? Take what back?"

"That there is such a thing as 'too much anime!!'" Then, stepping away, JP laughed and headed for A1A. "We should get back."

As they started to walk back to JP's place, Betty finally felt she could ask what she had been wondering about. "What is the situation with Steve? What happened to him?" Then thought, *That does not sound right,* so she added, "He seems very nice, but special."

JP held his head down towards the ground as they walked and spoke in a tone Sato had not heard him used before. "Steve is very nice. And what happened to him is Afghanistan. Same as what happened to thousands of perfectly fine young people. When will we ever learn? How stupid can we be? When will we ever learn?"

Betty knew this is not a topic to linger on. She could sense the mood had shifted and needed redirection. So, the tiny agent asked, "Do you need to get the dogs?"

"No, it's the routine, they finish the song and then lay down to sleep." JP turned back and also wanted to get back to happier thoughts, saying, "That way, I am free to go to the RC and get completely drunk and come home at dawn."

Sato had that sinking feeling not completely unlike a kid that finds out that those prints on the carpet were really the cat and not actually the Easter Bunny. Shyly, she asked, "You do that?"

"Well, I did once in 1997, didn't much like it, but one never knows when I might like to try it again."

'How can I ever know is when this guy is serious?' Sato thought as they crossed the road and turned south towards the RC.

# 11

## Betty reminds Joan of a raspberry

Looking forward to a bit more playful banter on the walk to the restaurant, JP was disappointed when the giant phone in his companion's hand started to shake and make a noise that sounded like a Pachinko game. The next thing he heard was a long stream of Japanese, he guessed. To be truthful, Jean Paul had been exposed to many languages, none of which were Asian. So, it could have been Mandarin, Thai, Korean, or whatever.

Japanese was a good guess, and it went on until almost their arrival at the RC. "Yaba yaba yaba yaba," moment of silence, then "Yabba yaba yaba yaba," silence, etc, etc. Then a final phase in a different tone: "yaba yaba." Upon which Betty looked at the face of the device and quickly typed several lines.

Betty said, "I am sorry about that. Important special project I am working on. And I may need your help, if you are willing."

JP spoke before thinking, still in play mode: "Anything for you, doll."

Too focused to be taken aback, shocked, curious, offended, or dozens of other feelings Betty could have experienced, Sato was getting to the task at hand. "How early do you get up in the morning?"

"That depends. Do you snore?" joked the deputy.

JP was taken aback, shocked, curious, and maybe offended by how quickly and forcefully this tiny thing put a right jab into his left shoulder. "Oh, that hurt" he yelped.

"Good! Now I have your attention. Will you help me? You just said you would!"

Getting into the uncomfortable demeanor of being serious, Barnett admitted, "Yes, I said I would, so I will. What's afoot?"

From the comment about 'A1A Irregulars' and the use of 'afoot,' Sato deduced that maybe Deputy Barnett was also a fan of the famous consulting detective. Of course, he probably did not set out to memorize each account at the age of five, like someone else did.

"5:30, be ready to go," the clearly determined female agent commanded as she quickly went up the restaurant steps.

"Holy shit, 5:30! The sun's not even up. I got up once that early and I clearly remember it was quite unpleasant."

Sato snapped around and pointed her small right index finger directly at JP's nose. "You promised!" Then Betty snapped back around even quicker than before and entered the RC.

Darryl was just finishing "Ain't No Mountain High Enough" and both the entering sleuths were surprised to see Williams actually smiling and appearing to have a good time. Approaching the table, JP was ready to throw out a smart remark, then the solo guitarist when straight to "I Heard It Through the Grapevine."

Martin held up his hand before Deputy Barnett could interrupt, signaling he wanted to hear this cover as it began.

As Darryl kept the crowd, including Williams, engaged, the two returning members of the law crew took their seats. About halfway through the song, Joan came up from behind Barnett and Sato and set down a lemon tart in front of JP and a raspberry one in front of Betty. Ms. Jett said, "I saved two," turning to Sato and putting her faceclose to that straight black hair. "The raspberry is for you, sweetness. You remind me of a raspberry."

Uncomfortable is not a strong enough word to describe how Betty felt, but she had too many parameters, contingencies, and even consequences racing around in her little head to even react. When the song was over and the desserts were almost gone, Williams, the tallest agent in town, stood up and appeared even larger than usual as he clapped loudly before turning to the rest of the group. "OK, it's time to go. We have an early morning."

"You are up before sunrise, too?" JP mouthed off, before being kicked under the table by a tiny foot.

"Hell no. I was thinking we would meet at your office at eight," said Martin.

JP bargained for more time. "Can we make it nine? I think I will need time to get ready."

Sato added, as if she was authorized to confirm, "Nine would be Much better."

Williams gave a disapproving stare and the junior female agent added, "I have some research I think I should do before we meet."

George felt like he should add something, but could not think of exactly what. Finally, he stated the obvious: "That dinner was fantastic, everything, even the rice was super. Wonder how rice can look so plain and be so delicious."

"It's white pepper and fresh lime, George," his boss tossed out. "My grandmother was found of white pepper. It has a sweet note to it." And with that Williams headed to the door.

The group moved to the stairs and out to the Jeep. "Where are the dogs?" asked George.

JP responded, "We left them at my house, so they could get to sleep early. Something tells me I will need to do the same."

The short ride to the Seahorse was breezy, and it actually felt the weather was getting a bit cooler. You never know what might happen in Florida, in March, along A1A.

# 12

# The Long Shot

JP let the dogs out to do their business as soon as he arrived home. Once they were all back inside, he hit the futon and was out like a light. Before the deputy knew it, softly there was *knock knock knock.* It felt and sounded like a dream, then louder. *Knock Knock Knock.* And then the sleepy headed lawman started to think, *Holy crap, is it 5:30 already?*

*KNOCK KNOCK KNOCK*

 "Ok, I'm up, hold on."

Pulling on his jeans and putting on a long sleeve shirt (as JP knew the weather had turned), he opened the door. Sato stood there in a gray jumpsuit with tennis shoes, a completely different look than the black suit with white shirt. "Let's go. I need you to get me to the hospital by 6:10. Can you do that?"

JP tried to focus and adjust to the light that Sato was shining at him from her phone. Slowly and lowly responding, "Sure, are you alright? Why the hospital?"

"I am fine. This is the task I need to do. And I need your help, as you promised," demanded the small woman holding the huge phone.

JP pointed to the motorcycle at the side of his house. "Want to get there quicker?"

"Let's please go in the Jeep," Betty said as she climbed into the passenger side of the Wrangler.

JP jumped in and headed North on the coastal highway, saying, "Are you going to fill me in?"

Sato responded, "My grandfather works in research at the University of Georgia. He is driving here from Athens with something he feels can help Carol Blink."

JP was really excited to hear this. "Really? What is it? Tell me all about it. This is great. I hope your grandad is right." Truly excited, as even though he knows it's not his fault, Barnett felt so bad this awful thing that happened to such a beautiful sweet girl on his watch.

Betty did not directly answer, but just added, "It's a six-hour drive from Athens and he is 87. Just hope he's safe. My grandfather is often right. I hope he is again. I need you to just promise to do what I say and follow my lead."

"Ok," assured JP, full of hope and a hundred questions.

Sato claimed her right of obligation. "I will take that as another promise." Then added, "By the way, I do find your Bonneville very interesting. It needs and deserves paint. What year is it? 1973 or 1974?"

JP was dumbfounded. He thought, *What the hell? This girl knows nothing about common things like otters or Michael Jackson, but spots the year on my Triumph?* He simply responded "1974."

Betty confounded the deputy even more. "Figures, that's the last year in the USA for a Triumph with right hand shift. I like riding motorcycles with a right-hand shifter. It's a nice change and so retro." She turns to him and smiled. "Maybe you will let me drive it sometime."

"You seem to know a lot about motorcycles, but are you sure you could handle that old Triumph? It's kind of a handful, quirky in many ways."

"Yes, I can handle it and even tune it if you need that done." Then added, "My father owned a motorcycle repair shop in San Diego. My sister and I always hung out there and learned to help, at least until Suzy decided to become a brilliant computer programmer." All of this statement except the *Yes* flew by JP, as he couldn't keep from thinking about Carol.

Exiting A1A, the Jeep headed towards the hospital. "How far are we?" inquired Betty, feeling the pressure of being on time to see her grandfather.

JP, still trying to take in this surprising discussion and their mission, said "Five minutes."

"Excellent. Remember your promise and follow my lead. Do exactly as I instruct," Sato said as they headed to the main parking lot of Flagler Hospital.

The parking lot was almost empty, as you might expect around 6am on a Saturday morning. At 48 degrees it felt much colder than it really was. Humidity can do that when you are this close to the coast. Sato pointed to an 80s-era Honda Accord, the silver faded paint looking particularly bad in the lights of the parking lot. "He is here already. Go over there."

JP parked next to the Honda as a small Japanese man bounded out of the car. *Wow, that guy sure doesn't look or act 87,* the deputy thought. Quickly Betty rushed over and gave the man a hug. The senior Sato opened his car's back door and pulled out two jars, which he handed to his granddaughter.

JP sat in the Jeep and observed and listened, as if listening would tell him anything.

The old man put his hand on the jar, which had a yellow top, and his other hand on the middle of Betty's chest.  They spoke a bit, then did the same routine, except he had his hand on a red-topped jar and other hand on the middle of the granddaughter's back, right above her butt.

They spoke and bowed. Sato turned to JP, saying, "Let's go," and she decided to throw in, "The game is afoot! "

Betty headed for the hospital with the deputy close behind, the elevator was on the main floor as you might expect with no one around. Once inside, JP got a good look at the jars and could only muster a rather loud, **"What the hell**?"

The jar with a yellow top had a sliding door in that top, and in the jar, there was a rather irritated acting large bee. The other jar had a similar door in its red top and within it was a very ominous looking hornet. JP stared at the jars and then squarely into Sato's face and repeated himself: **"What the Hell?"**

Sato commanded, "You promised to help!" Then she followed up with, "And this is not for me. In fact, it's a real risk for me. It's for Carol. I think it could be her only chance."

The deputy put everything together and then exclaimed, "What? We get her stung between her boobs and on her butt. This is some type of Voodoo? Voodoo in the hospital, that just sounds great!"

Sato protested, "It's Kampo, or it actually evolved into Kampo, but it's NOT Voodoo. And it could work. Plus, you promised!" Betty looked up at him with a face she was sure would get his compliance, but she was wrong.

It wasn't the female agent's expression that moved JP, it was his own thoughts: *Wonder if this could actually help Carol? Wonder if she had to be blind for life? Wonder if I could help her and I don't? If there is any shot, no matter how insane, I have to take it.*

"I am in," JP announced as the door opened and they head for 515. No one was about, even at the nurses stand, and they breezed right up to the door of Carol's room.

As Barnett reached for the handle, Sato handed him the red topped jar. "You put the murder hornet on the bottom of the spine, when I put the killer bee in between the breasts." Betty turns over her jar and hit the bottom with her fingernail, saying, "We tap on jars and hold tight to the skin until the bee dies. You slide the door back on top of the murder hornet."

"Murder hornet! Killer bee! Holy crap! It's insane. How will we control Carol?" JP started to think this girl FBI agent was actually beyond crazy, but he felt he's too far in to stop now.

"I will do that, and you back me up." Betty was clearly determined. She had given this a lot of thought and decided if she was going to break out of her mold, it should be for a cause beyond herself.

They opened the door and as they approached the bed, Betty commanded, "Take that chair and jam the door, just in case someone decides to come in." Sato approached the patient.

Leaning down, Betty gently shook Carol awake, as JP handled the door.

"What? Is that you, Mom? Did you come to visit again?" Carol whispered as she woke up.

"Ms. Blink, it's me, Agent Betty Sato with the FBI. I am here with deputy Barnett. We have some special treatment that is only known to a few in the FBI. I think it can help you, but it will hurt. I must let you know that. Plus, you must give me the authorization to use it."

"JP, are you here?" said Carol in a louder voice.

JP was unsure how to handle this, but kept running those what-if questions through his head. Deciding he was all in with this insanity, he responded, "Yes, Carol. I am here with just agent Sato. We are going to try to help you."

Betty brushed some blond hair away from its owners face, leaned down and whispered, "This is up to you, Carol. It will hurt, but I honestly think it might get you back your vision. Will you let us try?"

Carol nervously asked, "JP? Will you stay?"

"I will be right here, and I will stay," Barnett reassured the young blind girl, as he took his empty hand and gave Carol's arm a squeeze.

"OK, if I can see again, I don't care if it hurts," said the desperate girl.

Sato pulled the covers off and proceeded to instruct: "Lay on your side, facing me."
Betty took a piece of the sheet and pressed it to the blonde's lips.
"Open up your mouth and then bite on this."
"Now, try to breathe, and do not be nervous. This will really hurt bad for a few minutes, then you may get a small fever and some chills. You might throw up. You could get a bad headache and a loud ringing in your ears."

Luckily Agent Sato's normal duties did not call for a good bedside manner, and double bonus, it was lucky Carol could not speak with a sheet stuffed in her month.

Sato thought, *This girl has great breasts* as she let down the front of the hospital issue gown. Placing the jar top first between the best boobs she had ever seen, Betty signaled JP, who was already admiring an equally great backside.

Once in place, the jar handlers slid their doors out. The leader of this procedure whispered "GO" to her nervous helper. Instantly the beautiful girl undergoing the long shot treatment started whimpering and trying to scream while her body convulsions became more and more violent. Betty and JP both did their best with their free hands to control Carol's reactions.

The killer bee died fairly quickly, and Sato dropped her jar, which then broke at her feet, while she applied her full attention to keeping Carol from throwing herself off the bed. The murder hornet hung on and continued to deliver its venom to its only available target, and Betty yelled, "OFF NOW."

JP slid the door in as the hornet tried to escape. Once the angry insect was contained, the red jar was set on the nightstand. Barnett turned his attention to the bucking and crying girl, as her sheet was finally spit out and the loud screaming that erupted could be heard for at least the entire floor if not all of St. John's County. Shaking and pounding began on the door at once.

"Hold on, it's OK, I'll be right there," JP shouted as he headed for the door.

Once open, Barnett was not happy to see his old friend, the chief of medicine. Storming in, Dr. Cohen was followed by the taller of the two geek orderlies that had made the inappropriate visor remark. The doctor comforted his patient, who was withering in pain while moaning loudly. Pieces of broken jar lay on the floor with a dead bee. A jar on the table held a wildly buzzing hornet, his old friend with a terrified look on his face and that woman, that impertinent arrogant smart-ass woman!

Immediately walking to the girl in the bed, Isaac inspected the wounds on the chest and lower back, which he surmised must have been inflicted by these two amateur 'doctors.' Even though mindful of his duty to Ms. Blink, the only real doctor on the scene said nothing and left the orderly to attend to the patient. Marching straight into the hall, the chief of medicine turned and pointed to the intruders and motioned with one authoritative index finger to join him in the hall. Cohen had to know what had happened before he could proceed.

Once JP and Betty stepped out of the room, the doctor slammed the door and let loose. "What's wrong with you idiots? And JP, do you have any idea how stupid this is? Carol could be permanently disabled or worse! You could lose your job or even be arrested! Have you lost your mind? How did this vixen seduce you into this nonsense?"

Issac rushed back in the room and grabbed the red topped jar and stormed back to the hall. As the contents were inspected, Cohen called out to the nurses watching the drama, "Nancy, bring me diphenhydramine and a tetanus shot."

Not thinking of the trouble she was already in, Sato shouted, "Don't do that!"

Now enraged even more, the normally calm doctor said, "You arrogant little bitch, how dare you come in my hospital and practice witchcraft on my patient. You have no idea what the hell you are doing. Your stupid and backward actions are…"

Not willing to back off at this point, Betty interrupted, "Listen, Doctor Know-It-All, 3500 years ago when your tribe was using superstitions to escape enslavement, my ancestors had already been practicing and documenting medicine for 1500 years! Only a putz thinks he knows everything. You may find me arrogant and a bitch, but your chutzpah in assuming only your way can be right is meshuggenah."

Now the chief of medicine was not used to being talked to like that, except maybe by his brother, and his reaction was surprising even to himself. Isaac always thought of himself as open-minded. Even though he had celebrated how the plagues of Moses had convinced the Pharaoh to release the Israelites for as long as he could recall, Dr. Cohen could see how a Buddhist or a Shinto or whatever religion Betty was could see those plagues as myths.

On the other hand, the doctor thought, *Some homeopathic treatments seem to work. We don't exactly know why. Lots of people in France and Germany use homeopathic remedies. Maybe in Asia there are other folk cures that western medicine does not understand.* Collecting his composure, Dr Cohen said, "You should have at least run your ideas by the attending physician, and that would be me."

Sensing she might have a window to plead her case, Sato said, "I thought of that, but I guessed I would get nowhere. Maybe I was wrong, however. The establishment does have a vested interest in normality. I felt, and I think you will agree, no one held out much hope for Carol to get her vision back. I was guessing the plan was ease her into the idea of being blind for the rest of her life. Tell me if I was wrong."

As Isaac lowered his head a bit, he admitted as much without speaking, but he did have to defend his profession. "You should have cleared this idea with me, and if there was evidence of a possible alternative treatment, that could be studied."

Betty took her best shot. "There was no time for that. Optic nerve damage is hard to reverse, and my estimate was evidence is not something you might accept." She stepped closer to the doctor and looked up directly into his eyes. "Fugu fish improperly prepared by a boy in

1940 brought on almost instant nerve reaction and close to death. The boy was saved by a local 'witchdoctor' [using air quotes]. In Kochi there was not much room for modern emergency medical care."

Starting to feel how sincerely the young agent felt she was trying to help, sympathetically  Isaac pointed out, "Local legends from Japan from the last century are not what we normally base treatment on."

Still in the mode of driving home her case with one more bit of 'data,' Sato continued, "That boy was my grandfather, and he survived. Today he does research on insect, reptile, and fish venoms at the University of Georgia in Athens. I consulted with him, as I felt he had, may I say it, an open mind and the expertise that might help Ms. Blink."

Betty got lucky: Three times at the plate and three home runs! Speaks Yiddish, honors grandparent, and mentions UGA. Had she seen the bulldog stickers on the back of the doctor's Jaguar when she came in? No, it was just a lucky coincidence. Also, there was no way she could have known the doc always wore red and black underwear, or that he had season tickets for all University of Georgia football games since 1989. The super fan turned to his friend. "JP, why don't you go check on Carol?" And opened the door a bit in a manner that required no response.

Last thing the deputy heard from Cohen before he entered room 515 was, "Now, what about the fever, how high do you think it can go before I have to…"

# 13

# You're bat shit crazy

As the door closes behind him, JP cannot help but wonder how much trouble he could be in. *Could I be fired? That would not be so bad. Don't need the money anyway. I could work on my surfing. Could I be arrested? Maybe, but who would do it? I have friends, like Sheriff Richardson and the DA and Dr. Cohen. Maybe I would have to flee and take that job my father has offered for years at 'Le Submarine Americana.' But wait, no surfing in Paris! Maybe I could flee to Costa Rica.*

The last refrains of a familiar song interrupted his fanciful mental wanderings. The singer stood up quickly and acted in an awkward fashion that geeks specialize in. "Sorry, sir. I was waiting for you to get back so I could attend to my rounds. "

JP stepped up and pulled the sheet up to cover the mostly exposed naked body of Carol. "You do that." Then, turning to the patient, "Carol, it's JP." Sitting down and holding her hand. "How are you feeling?" JP noticed the drops of sweat on her forehead and that she was shaking like a rabbit who had been cornered by a coyote.

She laughed and sounded much better than she appeared. "JP, I know it's you. Of course, I know your voice. It's not too bad, as long as I lay on my side." Squeezing his hand, a bit. "Hey, you know about music. Do you know about that type of music where there are no instruments and people just sing?"

"Yes," the encouraged deputy responded.

"Is that called cold play? Or is that music with stuff like a guitar without electricity, is that cold play?"

JP was mystified. What could he say, except, "What?"

Carol said, "Just wondering. That doctor who was just here, sang me a song he wrote for me. It was beautiful." Ms. Blink did not realize the orderly was just claiming to be a doctor to impress her, but Barnett did.

"Really?" Very interested in music himself, Barnett wanted to hear more about this.

"Yea, I think he likes me. I hope he's cute." Carol smiled for the first time in a while, "The song went 'I wrote a song for you / And all the things you do / And it was called yellow.' I don't know what it means but it was beautiful. He said it's cold play, so I guess he doesn't know how to play like a real guitar. Doesn't matter, I wish I could…"

With very mixed emotions, JP knew he had to interrupt and see if he could keep things looking up. "Yes, he is cute. I guess, although you know I am not really into guys."

Carol laughed as JP continued, "Now, I am not saying there's anything wrong with that, just that guys don't appeal to me. But come to think of it, a young, tall, doctor, that's cute, and can sing, maybe if you don't want him, I will consider switching teams."

Laughing out loud by now, Carol screamed "Stop it, that's crazy, you going gay."

Just then the door opened and Dr. Cohen stepped in and gave JP a curious look and said, "Really? We can talk about this later," then the doctor reached over and put his hand on Carol's forehead as much to reassure her as to feel her temperature.

JP looked back at the door where Sato was standing. She smiled and mouthed without a single word, 'Gay?' and pointed at him. Shaking his head side to side, JP said, "It's a long story" with no attempt to suppress the volume.

Doctor Cohen addressed his patient. "Agent Sato has access to special experimental treatments that might help you, but there are no guarantees. Plus, since this is a special treatment, you may have some side effects, like chills, or a fever, or nausea. I normally leave on Saturday about noon, but today I will stay as long as I need to. I will leave this buzzy thing tied around the head of the bed. Push the bottom if you feel you need my help."

Carol dutifully replied, "Thank you doctor, I will. Thank you so much."

Standing and walking to the door, Cohen made a complete hand motion to JP as he passed Sato. JP said, "We all love you, Carol" and walked through the door. Closing that door behind him, the deputy got ready to be read the riot act.

"What you two have done is totally bat shit crazy," Doctor Cohen started in a newly calm voice, almost introspective. "About two years ago Rabbi Levi answered a question by telling me 'If you are driving home, and see a column of smoke coming from your neighborhood, and you do not wish that's it's not your house that's on fire, then you might be a good person.'"

JP and Sato looked at each other and then turned back to the freshly philosophical physician as he continued after a small pause. "The two of you took on great risks to your careers, and to everything you hold dear, not for personal gain, but to help someone else. Don't get me wrong, it was stupid, but in my heart, I hope there is something we have left to learn, even if from a fish."

Both men were shocked when Betty rushed into the doctor and hugged him. Sato then released and headed for the elevator. Before following, JP stuck out his hand, and it was met with the standard response, no parting words required.

# 14

## More cinnamon buns at the Annex

Silence and solitude were never easy on Jean Paul Barnett, and the trip down the elevator, out to the parking lot, and into the Jeep where less than fun. As this is a guy that was used to focusing on entertainment, and to be honest being the center of attention. By the time he returned to the Jeep, Barnett was sick of the lack of interaction.

"What did you and Isaac talk about while I was in with Carol?" asked JP.

"Lots of stuff," Betty responded, although she was not really ready to chat, thinking about what she had done and might do, and what's the point.

"Stuff is a broad topic," and with no response, JP added, "I had some really cool stuff when I was a kid. I had a Hulk action figure that could be put in hundreds of positions. I also had a mini foosball table, kid sized. I loved playing that. The kids…"

"OK, OK, we talked about his son and his son's career, my sister and her career, my mother and her cancer, my grandfather and the University of Georgia, the Exodus, and Kublai Khan, but mainly we talked about Carol and you."

"What? There nothing going on between Carol and me. Isaac knows that. Don't be sick."

"Actually, there is something going on between you and Carol. Doctor Cohen explained that fully. It's between YOU and EVERYONE in Crescent Beach. I would say Isaac is even a bit jealous."

Now JP was struck with the uncomfortable feeling of not knowing what to say next. "Hey, I wonder if we will get some time to catch some sleep before your boss wants us to continue." (He almost added "the wild goose chase," but thought better of it.)

Betty turned to Barnett and smiled. "You might. I will need to do a bit of research to convince Martin that starting late was justified." By the time they pulled into the lot of the Seahorse Inn, there was a light in a window. JP wondered if that was Williams' room. Betty knew it was.

Returning to his house, the deputy tried to catch a bit of sleep before getting up, waking up Steve, getting some cinnamon buns at Percy's pastry, heading to the Annex, etc. But it was no use. JP could not sleep after what all had happened in the last two hours. So, Barnett started his routine early. Won't hurt Steve to be up, plus those cinnamon buns sounded really good right about now.

Feeling like he was early when he entered the Annex, JP was a bit surprised that the FBI triple threat was standing in front of Mary's desk having coffee.

"Good morning, JP. You are early. I see you went to Percy's. Would you like a coffee?" asked the Annex's only other employee.

"Good morning, Mary. No thanks, I had one at the bakery. But I brought a half dozen cinnamon buns, so everyone can have one." The deputy set a white to-go box on the desk and flipped open the top. Instantly George stepped forward and picked one up and started to enjoy the best pastry north of the keys. The other two agents and Mary each picked one up, but only Mary started to eat at once.

Williams was, as always, in the mood to take control. "Deputy Barnett, I have arranged for Sheriff Richardson to meet us here at ten. So, I am glad you are early. We can discuss matters in your office until ten when he arrives."

Mary giggled and the special agent gave her a curious look.

Barnett knew why she was giggling and said, "Andy might be here by 10:30 or so. Mary, he won't be in the best mood, since his Saturday golf game with the judge and their 'caddies' is being disrupted. Please save those extra buns for him and make sure you have some hot coffee ready." Then JP turned and headed to his office, while saying, "Come on, let's go."

Of course, first on his heels, Sel and Poivre were where they knew they belonged. At least two of the agents following were not so sure. Once entering the office and turning on the lights, the three regulars took their places. One behind his desk and two on the floor. The Federal agents sat down in order by rank, which also matched height.

# 15

## Sheriff Richardson explains all

Deputy Barnett started the meeting off. "Did you notice all the lights in the Annex are LEDs? I changed them out two years ago when Andy had extra operating money that he wanted me to spend. I was so shocked at how much it reduced the electrical bill that I convinced dozens of local stores and restaurants to change over."

Agent Gonzalez said, "I thought it saved a little, but took years to pay off."

"That's what people say, my friend, but here's the secret: it's about the heat. Normal lights put out so much heat that your AC is fighting the lighting all the time. It's a bit cool today, but about 300 days a year we are running the air conditioning. The electrical savings pays for the LED in a season."

Williams had enough of this. "Fascinating, and I am sure we could talk about how to address climate change all day, but we have a job to do here. Which, if I can remind you, is to catch the unsub before they can strike again, and get them turned over to the judiciary."

JP snapped, "That's only one alternative."

Williams looked at him authoritatively. "The reason I requested Sheriff Richardson meet us here today is, I think your casual attitude is holding the investigation back. And I would like more local help. St. John's County has a rather large sheriff's department, and I feel it would help to have more manpower on the case."

"Manpower? What about woman power?" The joker in the room turned to Betty and winked. "Or maybe you just misspoke. I am sure the bureau does not condone gender-specific terms that can be offensive."

The special agent started to snap back, but thought better of it. Williams felt like he had the upper hand after talking to the assistant director and Andrew Richardson just this morning. Instead, he coolly said, "I am sure that Sheriff Richardson will agree with my assessment of the situation once he arrives and I explain it to him."

Noticing that JP is looking at George and smiling, Williams said, "Agent Gonzales, would you care to open the discussion on narrowing suspects while we wait for Sheriff Richardson?"

"OK, we feel that the events must have been planned for a while, so the unsub is likely local or lives in an adjoining town." The Latino looked at the dogs just for no particular reason then turned back towards his female partner. "Agent Sato has concluded the explosive was Tannerite, which takes planning, and the poison would have been planned out too. The shooting could be random due to incidental access to the gun, but likely someone knew where the truck with the rifle would be parked and when."

"Um hmm, I see, well I don't see it that way. Because I know it's not someone from Crescent Beach," JP said while staring up at the ceiling, reclining in his chair.

Betty inquired, "How can you be sure? It seems to me...."

Just then Andy Richardson walked through the door carrying a white take-out box in one hand and what's left of a cinnamon bun in his other hand. "Hey JP," said the short, somewhat round older lawman, dressed to play golf. "Percy is the best. I am glad I don't live too close to his bakery." He looks down at his own belly. Then Richardson turned to the agents. After a quick look over, he stuck out his hand. "You must be Special Agent Williams."

"Yes, sir. And this is Agent Gonzalez and Agent Sato," responded the lead Fed.

Richardson shook hands with both the junior agents as Williams started to fill him in: "Sheriff Richardson, my team feels that the investigation we have here could use more horsepower. There is a lot of ground and leads to cover. With your resources in the county, we were hoping we could get the operation expanded and we could set up a command center here at the Annex. That's why I called the assistant director and had him contact you."

"So, you do not feel like JP has enough help? Is that what I am hearing here?" asks Richardson.

The agents all looked at each other, and then the lead special agent replied, "It seems Deputy Barnett has no help. And to be honest, although he clearly has a knowledge of the area and the civilians, he does seem to have an overly casual attitude about the whole matter. We have a larger FBI team due to arrive Monday afternoon, but in the meantime, we would like to get more of your staff from Saint Augustine down here to help right now."

Sherriff Richardson looked at the box he was holding and thought, *I better save this bun for at least later today.* "JP, do you need more help to wrap this up?"

"Andy, I have 763 people on it now. I would think that's enough," the deputy stated clearly.

The FBI agents looked back and forth at each other, equally surprised at how quickly the Sheriff turned around and snapped at JP, "What? You don't have 989 people on the case?"

Barnett quipped back, "Andy, I am not counting anyone under 13, except the Chen boys, and the Russell and Jackson families are on a cruise, and of course, I would never count Ebo Walker, no way he could help." Both JP and the Sheriff started to laugh.

Deputy JP Barnett then added, "You said you wanted this concluded by Monday. I told you that is pressing it, but I agreed. Do we still have a deal or not?"

"I always do what I say. You get this bitch by Monday and you get an added member here at the Annex. Although I have no idea why you need that, but that's the deal."

Sheriff Andy Richardson turned directly to Martin Williams, looking him as straight in the eye as he could, given the almost one-foot difference in height. "Let me tell you a little story, Agent Williams.

"About four years ago, this arrogant jerk walks in my office wearing what seemed to be a surfer outfit that belonged on someone half his age. He said he can solve a series of rapes of Flagler college coeds that have been going on for about nine months. But he wants me to assign a detective that he can contact to make the actual arrest.

"I told him that's not the way things are done. He said OK, and calls me an ass. Then this jerk just storms out of my office. Three days later he shows back up with a local insurance salesman in tow, walks into my office at the objection of my secretary. And before I can throw them out, the insurance guy confesses to the rapes. The self-appointed detective just turns and walks out."

Richardson took a breath, looked at the uneaten cinnamon bun, then continued, "Well, fast forward about a year, me and the Missus walk into a bar on Saint George Street and there is a three-person steel drum band, a really good black woman singing, and a Rastafarian guy and a white guy on the steel drums. Damn they were good. But that's not the point. The white guy is the rape-solving prick.

"So, at the break I ask him to join the wife and me for a drink. Just to thank him and maybe request a song. During the conversation, I mention we are working on the sad case of a boy and his father being killed by a hit and run driver. Probably I mentioned we had no leads or something. And I tell him it's in Crescent Beach."

Andy looked over at JP as he moved the story along. "This guy, arrogant as ever, said he will give it a shot, if I give him an office to work out of. And since there was only Mary here in the Annex, I gave him this office and here he still sits."

Agent Williams looked away from Richardson's stare towards JP. "I guess I am going to assume the hit and run was solved."

The Sheriff barked back, "Damn straight it was solved. JP walked a very well respected, well connected, rich gentleman from Boston with his lawyer into my office three weeks later. He announces I need to have the DA come over so we can make a deal. About four hours later the entire matter is taken care of in a way that I would say was fair and beneficial to everyone."

Continuing on, Andy added, "Since that time, there's been no issues in Crescent Beach except me gaining thirty pounds, mainly from JP getting me to come down and eat at that cursed restaurant." He laughed and patted his belly.

JP had to throw in, "Violibobs tonight, Andy."

"I knew you would say that, but I already promised the Missus I would take her to the St. John's town center for shopping this afternoon, and then to a movie and dinner. Date night for old folks!"

Not giving up on getting the Sherriff down for a meal, Barnett announced, "There will be something really special, Andy, this Sunday brunch at the RC. I really want you to come. Bring your grandkids, I promise it's going to be worth it."

Agent Williams saw he was not breaking through the 'good ol boy network,' but wanted to enforce his position. "So, Sheriff Richardson, what I hear you saying is, if this investigation is not over by Monday, you will support my suggestion by supplying more manpower."

Richardson reassured the lead FBI agent quickly, "Yes" with his head a bit tilted down, either because he would not want to see this little beach community covered in his police, his detectives, and a bunch of Feds all dressed like corporate lawyers, or maybe he was just thinking about that box with Percy's masterpieces in it. Either way he felt he had to repeat it, "Yes, if it's not settled by then, I guess we will have to turn this town into a circus."

JP could not bear the thought of that. "Andy, that's not going to happen!"

Richardson felt he needed to assert some professional supervision in front of the FBI agents. "JP, for now, can you tell me if you have any good leads?"

Taking out his phone, it looked like Barnett was going to read a list of leads he had. Actually, he was texting Mary. "Sure, Mary is keeping a file on leads. I will have her bring it in."

Within about sixty seconds, Mary walked in with a big smile on her face and a notebook in her hand. The spiral notebook looked like it had belonged to a 4th or 5th grader, because it had. LARRY CARSON written in black marker- block letters on its blue front cover which was otherwise covered with stickers of race cars, motorcycles, surfboards, and one sticker of Batman.

It made total sense to Mary that there would be no reason to throw out a perfectly good notebook that had only about a fourth of the pages used. It made perfect sense to Williams that this completely amateur operation would have an untrained 'secretary' catalog and detail important criminal investigation information in something from a child's elementary school.

Feeling proud to be included in the group, Mary moved to the center of the front wall between the Barbets, so everyone could see her. Opening the spiral to a page with a small orange tab on it, she began: "What we know from the five eyewitness accounts is, the suspect is likely 5'6" to 5'8". She could be as short as 5'4" if she had worn platform shoes. However, I do not think that is the case, as one of the two co-eds was fairly certain she had on flip-flops. It is likely she wore a wig. The reason I think so is simple. Carol did not mention any dark roots when I asked. There are few true blondes and few women who dye often enough to show zero roots."

At this point, Williams was thinking, *Why didn't George ask about that? And actually, why didn't I think about it?*

Continuing on, Mrs. Carson summarized, "This woman has longish fingers and wears fake nails. Both Carol and the co-eds noticed now perfect her nails were. Typical red, not too long, but in perfect condition. It is very hard to keep natural nails in that good of shape."

Now Williams was sure: his team needs access to the co-eds, and frankly he needed to get his team refocused on these types of details. Putting his hand up just a bit, "Excuse me, Mary, how did you get this type of information from the college girls?"

"Easy. When I heard from Jason that he saw a boat explode, I texted JP, then I rushed down to the intercoastal. By then the four kids were onshore and I talked to the girls, while JP talked to Ron and Don, until the fire department came. And by the way, the suspect is rather shy or self-conscious about her body. Carol said she had on a long-sleeved shirt and long flared pants. Plus, she was wearing a bra, although she is rather flat chested. One of the co-eds said she noticed a one-piece black bathing suit under the beach cover up."

Looking around to see if everyone was actually interested in what she was saying, Mary was delighted that they seemed to be. So, she continued, "Also very interesting, the suspect who all the girls guessed to be in her late 20s to early 30s, has almost no facial lines or even a bit of tan. Which leads me to think she is not only not a local, but might not be from Florida."

Williams had to interrupt. "I am sorry, again, but why do you not think she's not a local?"

"First, Carol and the Gordon boys did not recognize her. Second, the suspect would have to be nuts to talk to Carol or the Gordons, cause they might have seen her before. Plus, third, everyone in Crescent Beach loves it here and would not want to make trouble." Williams felt she was joking about number three, but she absolutely was not.

"I asked Carol about the woman's earrings, asked the college girls too, but they did not remember, likely due to being drunk. Funny thing, Carol didn't exactly remember, but she said she thought they were golden leaves that covered most of her lower ear lobe. Might be nothing, but most women that age around here use studs and have at least two in each ear. Another reason I think the suspect might not even be from Florida or live on the coast. Plus, get this, she had an all-leather brown handbag, medium size. Who carries something like that? And what's the point? Leather bag on the beach. That's just my point of view. "

Richardson saw this going on for much longer than he had planned for. There was a chance of a little time on the driving range, before 'date night' with his wife. "Mary, that sounds very reasonable and well thought out to me. Do you have any suspects? Someone we can look into?"

Mrs. Carson was very encouraged by the Sheriff's comments, and she was determined to give a good showing with her list of women she felt could have done these awful things. "I have five on my list. I will go through them and tell you what JP and I are doing about it now.

"One, Jennifer Waterson, fits the build and age. She has short brown hair, but she could be wearing a wig, like I said. She and her husband live in Orlando, they buy and flip houses. Get this! She has been in Crescent Beach a lot trying to buy houses. Maybe she thought that by making us seem risky, prices of houses could be driven down. JP called the Sherriff in O-Town to check her out."

Deputy Barnett breaks in, "I actually called a detective friend of mine in the police department, and I asked him to run by and see if she has an alibi for Wednesday and Thursday. Seems she and the hubby are on a little road-trip vacation, and they told the neighbors they would be back Sunday night."

After JP signaled to proceed, Mary did just that.

"Two, Tara Gober, from Jacksonville. She fits exactly, Blond, 5'7" or so, right build. She was in Crescent Beach during late February trying to sell local businesses insurance. Of course, since everyone has been dealing with Oscar on that type of insurance for years, she got nowhere. Percy had kept her card; I called the number and there was a message that she was taking off March and would be back early April. I call that fishy."

No one had any questions, so, Mary just carried on.

"Three, Hazel Connor, also a good fit physically. She was a substitute UPS driver from Feb 14 to Feb 28, while our regular guy, Keith was taking off. This Hazel was not too friendly, if you ask me. Plus, it's likely Carol, Don, and Ron never saw her, as almost all UPS goes to businesses since Amazon started sending their own trucks to people's houses. Anyway, I called the supervisor at UPS. He said she had taken off March 1st to March 10th, to visit her mother, but he didn't know where. So, we can talk to her when she gets back."

Williams observed, "Maybe, but an employee of UPS I find unlikely. And what about motive? Does not make sense to me."

Barnett countered, "Motive is likely, that whoever it is, they are just a horrible harlot, or terrible tramp, or wacked-out wench. Just someone that wants to hurt people."

Williams acknowledged, "That's definitely a possibility. But at the FBI we have found most of these crimes are driven by a clear motive."

Sensing that the others were through commenting, Mary goes on.

"Fourth, Pamala Moonee, who is a perfect match in the size and appearance department. A bit older, but could look younger with a bit of makeup. Lives by herself, with like a dozen cats in Saint Augustine. She was in the RC last Saturday night and got no action, if you know what I mean. She works at home doing something online. I took the decision on my own to ask Evan Small in the Sherriff's Department to swing by and ask her a few questions. I hope that's OK, Andy."

"Of course, that's why we are there," said Richardson.

Mary smiled as she felt more part of law enforcement than ever. "So, Pamala tells Evan that Wednesday afternoon she went to the Orange Park mall. And that all day Thursday she was in Gainesville walking around campus, just hanging out.  Does any of that sound right to you guys? It sure doesn't to me. Who goes to the Orange Park mall anymore? She has no receipts and said she didn't buy anything. And why would a mid-thirties woman go hang out at UF? I talked to Evan about this and we have an idea, if it's ok with Andy."

Sheriff Richardson asked, "What is it?"

"I thought if Evan could go view the video surveillance at the Orange Park Mall, we could rule Pamala out, or maybe establish she might be lying. Evan has arranged with the mall to do it this afternoon and all day tomorrow. He had the most current interaction with her, and would be best to do this, I think. But it would involve some OT, so I was thinking of asking you today anyway. Is it OK?"

"Of course, please tell Evan to get on it. Great work, Mary." Andy saw the end of this visit in sight and pushed it forward. "Tell us about your last lead."

Mary had a big smile as she started to finish up.

"Fifth, AKA Linda, this unknown woman has been seen around Crescent Beach for the last week. She is a perfect match for the suspect that Carol described. But I could not get any info on hair roots or fingernails, because everyone that I can find that has seen her is a guy. They didn't seem to be looking at nails and such. No one knows her, and she doesn't talk much. Plus, two people saw a number tattoo on her right calf. That's kind of strange. Old Mr. Jenkins was on the beach Wednesday morning using his metal detector and saw this woman swim out of the ocean like at 6am. And, get this, as soon as she saw him, she started running south down the beach really fast.

"Then Thursday, about three in the afternoon, this woman walks into the Gas n' Go. She gets a Gatorade and a package of almonds. Randy Gliz is there at the register and tries to make conversation with her. He is the one that notices the number tattoo first. She seems to be breathing heavy and Randy said she was wearing a huge white T-Shirt, way too big for her. When Randy asks where she is from, she just puts down $5 and said 'keep the change.' Then she walks out.

"Friday evening, lots of people see her about 9:30 at the RC. She walks in, wearing an unflattering loose black pullover dress and running shoes that are like lime green! Looks around and just turns and leaves. No one recognizes her, but Dan Jenkins notices this strange tattoo. AKA Linda hasn't really spoken to anyone. Very strange, but that's all I know about her."

Williams found this account interesting, even though not too specific, inquiring as he feels Mary is through, "That is an interesting suspect. Can I ask how you know her name is Linda?"

Mary looked at him in a puzzled manner. "Well, I don't know what her name is. I just called her AKA Linda, because there was a girl in my second-grade class named Linda Hood who was just plain mean. Once Bobby Park brought a bullfrog to class in a shoebox for show and tell. The frog got out and was jumping all over the classroom, all the kids were screaming and even Mrs. Littleton stood up on her chair. Linda and Bobby chased the frog around the room, and when Linda got close to it, she STOMPED on it! She is just plain mean."

"So, is this Linda Hood a suspect?" the lead agent inquired.

"Lord no! She's too old, too tall, and she has a big scar on her face that she got after poking a German Shepherd with a stick." Mrs. Carson continued, "I just used AKA Linda as the name for this unknown woman, cause I didn't know her name. Problem is, no one has any idea where she is. Could be she's in Cape May, New Jersey, who knows?"

Williams thought he was catching up. "So, 'Linda' is just your name for the unknown suspect. Why would you think she might be in New Jersey?"

Mary looks at him with complete curiosity. How could Martin not understand what she meant? "Agent Williams, what I mean is I have no idea where she is. She could be in Cape May, or Pigeon Forge, Tennessee, or Las Vegas, Nevada, or BFE. I just don't know."

Everyone now got the reference, except Betty, who looked down and typed "BFE" in her phone. Sherriff Richardson said, "It's a great start Mary. I am glad JP has you here to help him." Then, turning to Barnett, he said, "OK, stay after it, JP. I will try to come Sunday. Not sure about the grandkids."

Then Richardson turned to the FBI agents. "It's been nice to meet you guys. I am sure JP will be glad to continue working with you." Waving like he was driving off in a car, Andy Richardson walked out of the office. Mary followed him out, as she wanted to bend his ear before the Sherriff returned to St Augustine

# 16

## A surprising lunch

JP was ready to get out of the Annex. "Well, that about takes care of the morning. What do you guys want to do this afternoon? Any leads we should work on?"

The three FBI agents sat down in their chairs and the lead Fed opened up. "JP, we are fairly certain that the boat explosion was Tannerite, that was primed by a small amount of dynamite. I think we should track down where the unsub got both."

"Lots of places sell Tannerite," threw in Sato. "I have called several and no one has a record of a sale that could be our suspect in the last few months in this area."

"Have you tried Daytona?" asked the man behind the desk.

Betty responded, "No, I thought that would be too far out of the area, but I can get on the phone and start calling hardware and farming related stores."

JP stood up and said, "Don't bother. I think I can find out where this bitch, I mean unsub, got the stuff to blow up the party boat." Then, characteristically playing with his goatee, he continued, "Let's run by the RC and get lunch. It's a light one today."

Williams was getting impatient. "Can't we get to work without stopping to eat?" And he stood up and headed for the door. The other two agents stood up and followed, as they looked back to see that Barnett was not following yet.

JP slowly walked over to each dog, pet their heads and supplied a biscuit. "Well Barbets, some people you will find are harder to deal with than others. I guess we need to go get them and make sure they do not get into trouble." Their master headed to the door. Sel and Poivre followed close behind, as always.

As the deputy passed Mary's desk, she said, "Violibobs tonight," and got what she already knew back: "I would not miss it."

Once outside, JP yelled to Williams, "Come on, Martin. We are on the same team here. And I know you don't want to drive that Kia. Let's just go to lunch. We might learn something there, and afterwards I think I can take you right to the person that sold the explosives to your so-called unsub." Pointing across the street, "Let's go to lunch in my Jeep, then I will take you to find out where this Tannerite issue takes us."

Williams nodded and held his hands up as he started across A1A.

"I'll take that as time for lunch," the deputy said, as all five followed Martin to the Wrangler,  the two fur covered riders were let in the tail gate, before all the humans took their normal seats.

It was less than ten minutes before the entire crew was walking in the front door of the RC. Not too different than lunch yesterday, four reporters at one table, four older ladies playing cards at another, and assorted people at the bar and a few tables. Nothing of note as the dogs took their place under the pool table, except Donna was up on a chair writing on a chalkboard that hung on the wall over Edgar's cage: "**Sunday brunch at 10:30 - Families Only - Reservations Required**."

Turning to see JP and his guests approaching their table, Ms. Reed hurried down off the chair, temporarily catching the bottom of her typical Saturday poodle shirt on the decorative edge of the bird cage. Momentarily the dress was in a position no lady would welcome.

Arriving at the crew's table, Donna said, "I hope I didn't expose you to anything you should not be seeing."

George popped off, "Only the fact that you put on the wrong day of the week underwear," and smiled a smile that was erased after he caught the glare from his boss.

Donna moved in close to the Cuban. "Well, it might not be wrong, because you don't know what day I put them on, do you?"

Sato opened her mouth a bit and stuck her index finger in it. Williams gave in and had to laugh. (Which was probably appropriate given that the underwear said "Wednesday" and it was Saturday morning)

"Donna, my friends here are in a bit of a hurry. Could you get Frenchie to expedite four lunches?" asked JP.

"Sure thing." She spun her shirt one and a half rounds and headed to the kitchen.

George started to ask about lunch, "JP, what is…." but was interrupted by a loud woman who stormed up behind JP and began to talk faster than anyone could almost hear. Most people on the Florida east coast speak somewhat slowly, however, Ms. Jane

Beauregard was an extreme exception. And the other exception was Jane's massive cleavage, which was by clothing design always in plain view.

*"JP, you wanted to know if anything weird is happening and I can tell you it is. Just this morning a lady came in and didn't pay any attention to these! Which is beyond strange, who comes into the ITT and does look at my tits? No one, that's who. Like these people here, the black guy is trying to be cool, the Asian chick keeps looking and then looking away, and this muscle man is like licking his lips. Of course, all guys look and women look even more, everyone knows that. Maybe once two years ago two gay guys from Key West came in and were not interested. I have no idea what was with them. They said they wanted a dress for their aunt, but I didn't believe them, whose aunt wears a size 4? Seriously. But that's none of my business, I don't care how they dress in their own private life. But I am telling you this woman this morning was a weirdo, she brought a simple dress and get this a coat that was too big, who does that? It's March, of course we are having a little cold snap, but buy an oversized coat in March? It's freakin spring. So that security contraption you put in my shop, I went in the back and ran the tape back until I had a picture on the little TV of this tit-indifferent bitch and I took a picture of it on my phone,"* and she held the phone up to JP's face so close he had to lean back to focus on it while continuing, *"and who are your friends here and why are they dressed like there's a funeral? There isn't a funeral is there?"*

Williams held up his hand as if that would slow this stream of thought down. "We are with the FBI and…"

*"The FBI! Well I'll be double careful about what I say to you. I saw all about how you sent Martha Stewart to jail*

*cause you said she was a liar. She is a wonderful woman if you ask me. And I didn't think lying is against the law - but what do I know? But I can tell you if it is you should go arrest my cousin Henry, that guy lies for no reason all the time."*

Williams saw this might never end, so he made the move he believed would cut to the chase. "Madam, can you please just tell us why you are here?" JP spotted the major mistake and put his hand on his forehead as the answer took off like a rocket from the Cape.

*"Since you ask and you're with the FBI, guess I have to tell you. It started Nov 14, 1884 - my great great great grandfather Jacob Beauregard and his friend Paul Bergman decide to leave Atlanta and move to Cuba since the war was going bad. And it's a good thing cause General Sherman burnt Atlanta the next day. Great great great granddad and his friend were already on their way southeast when the fires started. They could see them at night from miles away. Once they got near to the coast of Florida around St Simons Island they headed south. Right before getting to the St. John's River they decided to spend the night by a small lake. Unfortunately, while taking a swim Paul was bitten by a water moccasin. It must have been a young one, cause it unloaded all its venom in one strike. An older snake would not get scared and do that. My great great great grandfather had to bury his friend and continue on"* (about this time Martin started kicking JP's left boot, which continued and increased as Jane kept going) *"and maybe it was ordained cause now he had two horses. So getting to the St. John's River great great great grandfather was able to trade the horse for a barge ride across the river plus ten dollars confederate. Several days riding south along the coast and of course stopping at the old town at Saint Augustine Bay to get some provisions with his ten*

dollars, he ran into trouble as most thought the money would be no good, but finally got someone to get him what he needed. Heading south past the bay, great great great grandfather decided to ride along the beach until he saw a beautiful and super well-endowed Seminole Indian girl fishing in the surf. So that is where my great great great grandfather and grandmother Jacob and Aiyanna meet and in time started a family right here in what became know as Crescent Beach. Of course, in those days…"

JP stood up after several minutes of Agent Williams kicking his left foot and grabbed Jane by the hand and walked toward the door.

*"JP, where are we going? I am not finished answering the FBI question of why am I here and…"*

The deputy said loudly, "Jane, it's important that you meet Mary at the ITT right now. She needs something from the shop and customers have been coming to get in and finding you are closed. So, you are missing business." (Which was likely not true, but who knows? It might have been the case.)

As the two neared the door, she said, *"OK, but if the FBI needs me to finish, let me know. And what does Mary need? I think you should send over that Asian girl, I have an outfit I ordered for early teen types that would look really cute on her. Maybe I will show that to Mary or send you a picture. It's great and…"*

"Please show it to Mary," JP said as they stepped through the door. He quickly turned around and re-entered the RC.

Barnett returned to the table right as Donna walked up with four plates with the same simple three dishes on each: wheat crepes filled with sliced meatballs and grated Parisian cheese, green beans, and small chopped Thai salad. "Looks great, Donna. Can you have Frenchie get the dessert ready ASAP? Like I said, my friends are in a bit of a rush."

"It's not natural to rush on Saturday, but sure thing, I will tell him now," Ms. Reed said as she turned around and headed back to the kitchen.

Williams sensed this was dragging on too long. "Really, I don't think we have time for a long meal, can the dessert wait or be to go?"

Before JP can object, George chimed in, "My god, you have to try this crepe, it's insane! How the hell does he make this?"

Sato said, "I haven't tried the crepe, but the green beans and salad are yummy. They have a smooth but spicy Asian taste, must be Korean or Thai, as it's certainly not Chinese or Japanese."

By now, JP was eating and had forgotten to respond to the dessert challenge, which Martin felt like retracting as he started on his crepe. The barmaid brought over four small cups of cider and sat one by each diner at the table. The discussion had stopped as the focus shifted to the Saturday lunch special.

Right on cue, Ms. Reed returned with four small plates that she replaced the main course plates with, as lunch was completed. No longer commenting on timing, Williams saw his dessert and observed, "Perfect. Crepes beurre sucre! Great choice. I need to meet this cook."

Last time Martin had crepes like these was in the Big Easy.

"Now you see, it's worth an extra ten minutes to finish lunch properly," said JP as he looked at the head agent. "And we will have time. It's only an hour to Daytona, so with the drive down and back, a couple hours to find and interview, we can be back in time for an important appointment this evening."

Ten minutes did not turn out to be enough time to finish. Sure, the crepes were gone in seven minutes (three for George). But one other matter had to be handled.

As the crew stood up to depart, a very excited woman rushed in yelling in JP's direction, "El diablo envio demonios a mi casa!" She locked in on the deputy. The new arrival, dressed in jeans and a yellow peasant top with colorful patterns around the neck, charged toward the crew's table. Again screaming, "El diablo envio demonios a mi casa!" halfway through the RC.

As she neared her target, the FBI agents took their seats, assuming this would be best sat out. Sel and Poivre left their posts under the gaming furniture, and appeared silently at the side of their master.

"El Diablo envio demonios a mi casa," the woman yelled directly in the face of JP, the one person she prayed could help her.

George had two thoughts at once: *(a) maybe this lady is crazy to be thinking and screaming that the devil had sent demons to her house and (b) this lady is so beautiful, her hair, her face, the sterling silver engraved earrings with perfect contrast against her lovely brown neck, and the way she fills out the top of those jeans.*

Gonzalez would like to help her himself, but she was laser focused on Barnett.

JP reached out and grabbed the woman's arms, then pulled her in for a long hug. Agent Gonzalez felt a bit disappointed by this as he heard Barnett say, "Catalina, you know I am here to help you. I will not let Satan threaten you or the boys." Then releasing the hug and stepping back but not by much, he said, "Catalina, first, where are the boys?"

Calming down and feeling a bit more at ease, the woman responded, "They are in the car," turning and pointing, "right outside."

"Are they alone?" asked JP at once.

The mother, now aware of JPs main concern for her 4 and 6 year-old sons, said, "I could never leave them alone, just like you said, JP. Steve was walking up and he said he would watch them."

This reassured the deputy, who was focused on 'to protect and serve,' even though he would never use that phrase. Proceeding to take charge, JP requested, "Catalina, you need to take the boys to the Seahorse. Check in for the night. Drive there with Steve just to be safe. Tell Alice I said to put you in room 116."

Looking closely in the woman's face, Barnett said, "Then I will take care of el diablo and his evil ways. I guarantee you Satan and his demons will be gone by Sunday before noon. And they will not want to risk a return anytime soon!"

Looking very grateful but concerned, she said, "JP, I am not sure I can afford such a fine hotel room. I love you for dealing with the demons, but maybe I can stay somewhere else."

"Catalina, it is the DUTY of the County to keep the Devil away. I will get the bill for the hotel handled, plus I will call Alice and have her get some chicken fingers and French fries sent for you and the boys."

The young mother threw herself on the deputy. "Gracias, JP, I love you." George wanted to be in a position to receive this type of gratitude, and maybe more.

JP saw that it was time to wrap this up and get details handled and help his guests waste their afternoon and get back to the RC for violibobs, his favorite.

"Now, Catalina, I need your key, then go with Steve to the Seahorse, and I want you and the boys to come back here tomorrow at 10:30. I will see to it that the county gets you a special RC Sunday brunch." JP turned to Donna, who was watching the spectacle from several feet away, and winked.

Catalina reached in her jeans pocket and pulled out a key that she handed to her hero, and kissed him on the check, turned around and headed for the door. Gonzalez hated to see her go, but he enjoyed the view.

Barnett informed the restaurant owner, "Donna, I need you to help me with this."

Ms. Reed said, "Just like last time, I assume. And, of course I will help. What's the list again?"

"I need two whole onions, two whole garlic bulbs, a large bunch of chili reds. Frenchie can get all that. Try to get a couple of small bibles and some of those little crosses from Reverend Green that they use at Sunday school, or maybe even better, Frenchie could go to St Augustine to the cathedral. Either way, when Steve gets here later, have him take the stuff to my place."

Donna nodded while taking all this in and responded, "You got it, JP. I will make sure it's all at your house before dinner."

JP stepped closer to Donna and said, "You are the best. This town is so lucky to have you here. Can you do one more thing? Ask Frenchie to make some violibobs early to give to Steve when he comes by."

Faltering and blushing, the woman with the retro style reassured the deputy, "Of course, and don't worry, I have it all under control."

JP turned to the astonished and bewildered FBI agents and called for action, "OK, let's get rolling, we are burning daylight." Then Barnett headed for the door with his four-legged companions right on his heels. Three Feds were close behind.

# 17

# The Road to Daytona

Sel and Poivre in the back and all FBI agents in their seats, JP fired the Wrangler up and reached for the custom brake lock, so he could dramatically spin the thing around with the left wheels locked in place. Williams put a large strong hand on his shoulder. "Please don't pull that trick. Just back out."

Sticking his lower lip out in a faux sad face, JP whispered "kill joy" as he gunned the Jeep in reverse, whipped it onto the street and headed for A1A.

The special agent had what seemed like a serious matter on his mind. "Can we talk about what just happened back there?"

The driver was ready to have some fun and followed up quickly, "Sure. It is amazing, isn't it? How does Frenchie think up these dishes? That is a fabulous lunch and not too heavy. I mean meatballs with cheese in a crepe, who does that?"

Before Williams could interrupt to change the direction, George piped in and kept it on topic: "I know! Completely delicious, and if you had asked me if I wanted that dish on a menu, I would have said hell no! But I was blown away."

Not normally in on this type of banter, Sato added, "Although I do not really focus on food that much, like some do, I have to say that was a really surprising meal.

The green beans were my favorite, maybe best I have ever had."

Blasting south down the coastal road, feeling very smug in his belief he could divert the normal questioning about the case, chilling breeze all though the cabin, JP was having a great time and getting ready for the inevitable. Mr. Serious Agent did not surprise the driver a bit with, "Yes, it was an excellent lunch, but I want to talk about the woman…"

Loaded and ready, JP interrupted, "Oh Jane, yes she is a handful. That lady can really talk. Sorry if you didn't get the entire history of her family since the Civil War. But I can fill you in on the next four generations, as I have heard it several times."

"Please don't," insisted Williams.

"Oh, so you want to know about her store. Funny, she rented the place twenty years before I was working here, and she put up a big sign that said 'It's The Tits Fashions,' which back in those days there were some more tight ass people around who demanded the sign come down…"

Williams was determined. "I am sure the evolution of the shop naming is fascinating, but you know what I want to discuss." Martin turned around in his seat and stared at Betty and George, then focused on Barnett, the guy trying to sidetrack the conversation. "Catalina, the woman who is clearly disturbed and maybe dangerous. I want to know why you are not bringing in social services and getting protection for her children."

Seeing the expression on JP's face make a 180 degree turn, Martin added, "I know this matter maybe local, and you might not see how the FBI could have an interest in it." Now noticing the driver's hands clench on the wheel, Williams interjected justification: "For all I know, she could be a suspect."

That did it!!! JP was having none of that BS. "Listen, you have no idea what you're talking about or what's going on here. You need to lighten up and mind your own business."

Williams was also starting to lose his cool a bit after being toyed with while attempting to get to the topic. "I know there is a crazy woman who thinks the devil sent demons to her house and you just sent her off with two minors and told her you would perform an exorcism in her home."

"YOU MAY SEE A CRAZY WOMAN, LET ME TELL YOU WHAT I SEE! I see a good woman who married an asshole loser that decided he was a hot shot gambler and went to Atlantic City, lost all their money, ran up a big debt, and got stabbed to death in a fight. I see a mom left with two great sons to support who gets up about midnight six days a week and drives to this place we are about to pass here on the left, the 'Hammock Beach Golf Resort' and works till 7:30am, and drives back to Crescent Beach to take care of her children. She makes sure all the sheets and towels and such are ready every day for SNOTS like you!"

"Hold on. I am sure she is hardworking and tries her best to be a good mother. I am just saying she is delusional and could be dangerous."

"WHAT? She's delusional because Satan sends demons to her house?"

The special agent is equally fired up. "YES. She is delusional and the way you are handling it is completely inappropriate."

There is a hierarchy in the FBI and these three agents were well aware of it, as the lead agent had made it crystal clear. Martin Williams was used to subordinates that salute and say "Yes sir." But something triggered Gonzalez to step outside the halo of authority and say, "Martin, MY mother believes in demons. You have no right to call someone with different beliefs crazy or delusional."

Williams was stunned enough that Sato, as always on her phone searching, tried to calm things down by commenting, "There are 1.3 billion Catholics. Most believe in spirits, angels, demons, and Satan." Seeing the disapproval in her boss's face, she realized maybe that wasn't the best thing to say. So, Betty added, "Of course, there are varying degrees of belief, and one could be Catholic and delusional at the same time." Now, she saw a super dirty look from Gonzalez. So, in an attempt to dig her way out, she drew on personal experience. "In Japan there is the Akuma, which is a fire spirit. Some would call Akuma a devil or demon. My grandmother used to tell me stories that had Akuma in them all the time. I loved those stories. My grandmother felt strongly that Akuma was a presence in life and could affect people."

Williams started to say, *Yes, but you do not think this fire spirit has invaded your apartment, and you don't run to the police for help about it,* but he could see this entire situation was headed in totally the wrong direction. He could not take on the entire Catholic Church, Japanese folklore, George's mother, Betty's grandmother, and who knows what else. Plus, his own grandmother had a

Voodoo shop with fortune telling on the side right in New Orleans. Time to back off this topic. It was going nowhere. Martin could be overbearing, but he knew when to cut his losses. "I am sorry JP. You are right, this is a local matter. Can you fill us in on how you have located who sold the unsub the Tannerite and the dynamite?"

Barnett was glad to move back to being in his natural laidback mode. "No problem. I understand, it's hard to stand by when you think something is amiss. As far as the source for the Tannerite and whatever ignited it, I have to admit I am not positive I know. But I am fairly sure who can tell me."

About then, the Jeep turned left on to Granada Blvd in Ormond Beach and was driven straight onto the hard-packed sand of the eastern coast of Florida. Driving quickly, the 4-wheeler whipped south along the beach. Even though it was a bit chilly and still just March, girls in bikinis were laying out on towels between where cars drive on the beach and the surf, a couple of college guys in baggies throwing Frisbees near the water. A food truck parked nearby, a bit off the traffic lane, touted 'snow cones and corny dogs.' All fairly tame compared to how crowded the beach from Ormond to Daytona is once summer hits. By June there will be hundreds of cars driving north and south on the hard-packed sand of the eastern Florida coast, with thousands of beach goers laying out, walking, and playing in the surf.

"What are you doing?" asked the guy riding shotgun, who had just had sand thrown on his pants leg from the sudden turn onto the beach.

"I am taking a shortcut," came the response, accompanied by a great grin and passive recognition that the side trip would not really save time, but would be more fun. "George, cover the face of the phone Betty is holding," and then a bit louder, "Now, Miss Smarty Pants, can you tell me why this beach is so famous for driving cars on, and about Barney Oldfield, in your own words?"

Sato looked over at Gonzalez, then down at the hand covering her resource center, determined to not sound like an encyclopedia. "OK, let's see." A pause, maybe for effect. "Daytona Beach and Barney Oldfield…" another pause as Betty continued to look down. "Maybe you are referring to Oldfield setting a land speed record March 16, 1910 on this beach of 131.72 miles per hour in his Blitzen Benz," then quickly thinking to herself, *I just should have said about 1910 and over 130 MPH. That would have sounded more natural.*

George said, "Wow, that's impressive. Not that you knew that, I assumed you would. It's impressive that they raced cars here and set speed records on the Beach. I always wondered why Daytona was famous for racing and has the international speedway."

Just then, the Jeep took a turn back west on to Sea Breeze Blvd, went across A1A and ended up in a small business district. JP slowed down and said, "Let's see, I think it's right around here." He turned on a large street that paralleled the main ocean road but two blocks west. "Ok, here we are."

He parked right in front of a cinderblock gray building, 100 feet wide, with no windows, and a solid metal door in the center with a red canopy over it. On the front giant neon letters read **THE REAR END** with a smaller painted-on message below: 'gentleman's club.'

Sato was somewhat surprised and let it show as she said, "You are taking us to a strip club called The Rear End?"

"Well, they tend to name things after car or motorcycle stuff here in Daytona. Sorry it's not the Moulin Rouge, but this ain't Paris." The driver started to step out, adding, "It's better if I do this alone. I should be right back. George, make sure my puppies are not molested."

Sato just commented, "You have parked in a handicap space."

"No problem. If the law shows up, just tell them you're with the FBI. And actually, if anyone comes out of the club and asks, flash your badges and just make it very clear the FBI may have business in the club." And with that, Deputy Barnett headed towards that solid metal door, behind which some feel they might find carnal pleasures.

# 18

## Quick trip to the strip club

Exactly as JP expected, The Rear End was a typical old school strip joint that had been slowly pulled through the decades. As he opened the door there was a little stand to the left with a sign on it that said "$5 cover after 6" and although no cashier was present since it was still afternoon, there was a big guy in an all-black suit with a red shirt, buzzed head, mustache, and generally menacing look that sent the silent message: "Don't mess with me. I'll hurt you."

JP stood next to the bouncer and took in the club : old guy with long hair and a beard that looked like he was from the 60s and in charge, sitting next to the DJ stand that was covered with red shag carpet from the 70s, in the ceiling a disco ball from the 80s turned as "Learning to Fly" by Tom Petty from the 90s mixed with the smoke in the air, and on the middle of three stages with poles danced a tall skinny woman in a g-string born in the 2000s. The Rear End clearly had half a century of entertainment and local culture covered.

Still feeling a bit confrontational after the dust up with Martin, JP almost started out with *Listen, meathead,* but his natural demeanor took over as he reached over and slapped the big guy on the shoulder. "Hey, I am here to talk to Logan for a bit. Could you do us a favor? Check on who those three yahoos parked in the handicap space are and let me and Logan know what they are up to." The deputy thought to himself, *I wish I could watch this guy try to shakeup Williams.*

As the Bouncer nodded and stepped to the door without a word, JP quickly walked through the assorted tables, which had only a few girls that were waiting for their turn to dance, past the bar which had only three men sitting, nursing drinks. Coming face to face with the owner, Barnett said, "Logan, I am JP Barnett, Sheriff of Crescent Beach. I was referred to you by a mutual friend."

Taking the half-smoked unlit cigar out of his mouth, he said, "Really? Who would that be and why are you here?"

JP had dealt with attitude lots of times. Luckily, he had an ace in the hole, or maybe it was more like three of a kind in a Wrangler. "Tasha Smirnoff and I need you to show me your floor video from Wednesday. Plus, I need you to tell me where in Daytona I could get some M80s."

Logan was used to local police looking the other way for cash, drinks, and/or favors from girls. And he could size people up very well after forty years in this biz. His take was, this guy was not going to be one of that type. Not sure what JP's game was, but this bar owner didn't want to play.

"Well, Sheriff, we have two problems. This is not your jurisdiction. Plus, you have no warrant, or you would have led with that."

JP looked over his shoulder as the bouncer approached. Without acknowledging who sent him out the front door, the guard said, "Boss, there are three FBI agents parked in front. And they are not too friendly. I asked why they were there, and the tall black one told me to mind my own business and if he needed, he would come in and see if there are any federal violations he can find."

Logan looked at JP, demanding to know, "What the hell is this?"

Nervously, the super big tough guy suddenly did not sound very secure. "Boss, I can't be dealing with the FBI. Can I take the rest of the day off? I could just walk out the back and come back tomorrow."

JP put his hand on the big man's shoulder for a second time. "Don't worry about it. You do not need to leave. Just go back to the door. Everything will be fine. Logan here was just about to help me out, then I will get those Feds rolling on down the road."

Calming down a bit, but still uneasy, the man paid to be intimidating returned to his station like a puppy that had been hit with a wet newspaper.

Answering the question that the proprietor had previously asked, "Logan, this is about something that does not involve you, or your business, or your employees. Those FBI agents are with me, and they wanted to march in here and cause issues that only the stinking feds can cause. But I told them that you and I could work it out. Two simple things, and I promise you will never hear anything else about this." JP knew that getting this guy on his side would make it easy. "Listen, Logan, I bet you don't want to deal with the Federal Government any more than I do. But YOU are lucky. You don't have to. I am stuck with them."

Logan mulled over his options and wanted a bit of reassurance. "So, all you want is to view my security video from Wednesday and for me to tell you where someone could get M80s, or I guess similar explosives?

After that, you and your 'friends' go away so I can get back to running my business."

"That's right. You have my word. That's all I need, and you won't see me again. Unless Tasha convinces me to come here to hang out and party." JP winked and gave the entrepreneur that specializes in leisure time diversions a big smile.

"Follow me back to my office," said Logan as he stood up and headed to a door that was between the bar and the DJ stand.

# 19

## Gonzalez can speak the language

JP emerged from The Rear End with a big grin on his face, which in a way disturbed Betty. Sending a text on his phone and walking to the tailgate, he pulled two biscuits from his jeans pocket. "Did George take care of you guys? You are good dogs." Two tails wagged wildly as treats were devoured.

Stepping quickly back to the driver's side, JP looked at Williams as he got in. "Wow, you must have done a great job introducing yourself to that bouncer. I think you scared him senseless."

The special agent just nodded, and when there seemed to be no verbal response, George interjected, "The guy made a bad mistake by storming out and getting instantly aggressive with Martin. I wish you could have seen how quickly Martin got out of the Jeep and backed that guy all the way to the front of the building." Laughing, Gonzalez added, "By the time Sato and I were out and headed that way, it looked like that idiot was about to pee in his pants."

Agent Williams, as always, wanted to move to the business at hand. "Did you get a lead on the source of the explosives?"

JP was already backing out as he started to address what he found out, at least the part that he felt the FBI either needed to know or that would distract them until he could finish his own research. "Yes, I think I know where this shrew got her supplies for the that boat trick. I am headed there now."

Martin, of course, wanted to know more. "Can you give us more details?"

"Sure, there is a guy with a little gun shop over off Speedway, right between A1A and the river. The place is called Deadeye Dick's and, big surprise, the owner and probably only employee is named Dick."

Sato said, "The river? How far is that?" and before she could get a response, George turned to her and said, "Once you get a little south, people start calling the intercoastal the river."

JP's response was direct: "That's right, George, cause on the first coast we also have the St Johns River, so we would get confused if we called the intercoastal the river. And lord knows we are already easily confused enough," to which only JP and George laughed a bit.

The small woman with the large phone in her face continued to a new topic. "Richard Harper, 51 years old, five felony assaults, one conviction, dozens of misdemeanors, mainly traffic. The felony arrests were two controlled substance, two disorderly conduct, and one assault."

JP looked at Williams. "She is hell on wheels with that phone, isn't she?"

He nodded and skipped to the important details. "This guy sounds like he could be trouble. We should make our overwhelming force clear when we enter his shop."

Barnett, the guy more familiar with the area, disagreed and said so. "He sounds like a typical guy in Daytona. Gets drunk now and then, or gets stoned. Gets in a fight or three in bars, speeds and runs some lights. Hey, it's Daytona. You do not want to seem threatening to this guy. He'll clam up."

George broke out laughing, and fueled by this, JP added, "Dick probably runs straight pipes on his truck or Harley." The laughter heightens, as do the theories on offenses. "Likely hunts deer out of season, and catches over the limit fish." At this, Williams turned around and glared at Gonzalez, who instantly straightened up.

"To be clear, what we need out of Mr. Deadeye Dick, is a full description of the vicious vixen and the time of sales and items. Assuming he's the source?" Deputy Barnett asked the group for confirmation.

Williams responded, "Yes, that should do it, and maybe a few other details," to which Betty added, "And if there is intel on the trigger device, amount of Tannerite, additional items, type of payment, any video surveillance, places where fingerprints might remain, and ID used."

As they turned onto International Speedway Blvd, they quickly saw the gun store on the left, which JP drove past as he interrupted Sato, "Whoa, that's too much. If I am going to get anything it needs to be smooth and limited. Otherwise, I won't get dick out of Dick." Both the male agents smiled, but this flew right past Betty.

Williams commented, "Why did you say 'I'? This is the type of interrogation that I should do. And why are you parking here?"

"I figured I would walk down and talk to Dick, and then if I needed you guys, I could call you," JP said while holding out his phone. "If we all walk in there, he is likely to not say anything or ask for a lawyer or whatever, and we won't get what we came for."

Williams stared up a minute, and then looked over and said, "Maybe you are right, but this should be an interview by the agency. I will do it by myself."

As the special agent got out of the Jeep, Gonzalez spoke up. "I should do it. It's a gun store, the guy is a gun guy. I can speak his language, no matter what he's into. Nothing against you, Martin, but do you see what I mean?"

The lead agent really wanted to do this interview, but what the hell, George had a point. Of course, Williams knew firearms, but nothing like George, who was a true enthusiast. "OK George, you have a good point. Go in and see what you can find out. Do look out. He is certainly armed."

While Gonzalez was getting out, Betty started to repeat her list of information to acquire, but thought better of it and just said, "Good luck."

As George headed away, JP called out, "I know you're a pro, George, but I suggest you take off your jacket and your tie. Put the guy at ease. It's Florida, remember."

After turning around and thinking one second, George did that and handed the two monkey suit articles to Betty. Then he untucked his shirt so he would look even more coastal, plus his side arm would be covered.

For about forty minutes, the two agents and the deputy sat in the Jeep, with the latter trying to convince the former they should go to the beach and take a walk. Once it was clear that the lead agent was not into the beach, JP suggested a drive over the river to the Harley shop to just kick some tires. No dice. The special agent was not interested in looking at what's new or custom with the iconic two wheelers. This back and forth on how to waste time went on until Gonzalez returned.

Upon entering the Jeep, George started out excitedly, "Dick has a Luger P08 parabellum in there that his father took off a Nazi in '44. And get this: he has an M1891 Mosin-Nagant 7.62mm with a PE scope, same as used…"

"Can we get to the case?," interrupted Williams. "I'm sure it's an interesting shop. But did this guy sell the unsub explosives? What did you find out?"

JP started the Jeep and backed out, heading back to Crescent Beach. And George filled everyone in.

"Dick did sell a woman some Tannerite and some M80s, plus a remote to set it off. He described her almost exactly the same as Carol did, down to the clothes."

It would take many more details to satisfy Betty Sato.


*Sato:* "What about the security system?"
*Gonzalez:* "It's a super old tape that rewinds every 24 hours and then records. But worse, it's broken. I suggested Dick get a new, modern system."
*Sato:* "Any surfaces where there could be latent prints?"

*Gonzalez:* "Dick's mother, who is 73, goes in everyday for lunch. She brings it in. And she must be super type A, because she cleans everything every day. That place is spotless."

*Sato:* "And how did the unsub pay?"

*Gonzalez:* "Cash. Dick only takes cash, and his mother deposits it every day after lunch."

*Sato:* "What about ID records? Did he photo her DL and have her sign a form?"

*Gonzalez:* "Dick screwed up. This woman charmed him, said she'd just bought a house in Ormand and she needed to blow up a stump that was full of ants. He saw an ID and all he remembered was the name was Amber Green and the state was Ohio."

JP weighed in at once. "So, we know for sure this wench is not from Ohio and is not named Amber Green. Betty, please do your search and eliminate everyone called Amber Green in the USA, and all women from Ohio."

Not laughing, Williams added, "One thing we know for sure: Dick has violated several state and federal laws. We can deal with him next."

George was a bit taken aback. "I promised the guy, if he helped me, he would not be involved in our prosecution as long as he was not directly linked to the crimes we are looking at."

The lead agent pointed out, "Luckily, it's OK for us to lie. Good job, George. Include all the details and give me a report."

JP didn't like the direction here. "You know, we have the best sketch artist in Saint Augustine. Nancy Watson, she was doing drawings for tourists in the old town. You know, the caricature type. Anyway, Andy had her do one of his grandkids, and he was so impressed, he hired her. It's a part time gig, but we could get her to meet up with Dick and end up with picture that I bet would be dead bang."

Williams agreed and said, "I guess we can leave it to the locals to handle Dick later. A picture would be great. That would give us a real shot of solving this quickly."

Feeling good, both George and JP were glad the focus on the gun and sometimes illegal fireworks seller had been at least postponed. Barnett felt sure he could get it completely derailed and he could scare Dick later into cleaning his act up.

Heading north on A1A with an impressive late afternoon view of the Atlantic Ocean on the right, the conversation lagged until approaching Crescent Beach. JP suggested a little change. "How about you guys lighten your wardrobe up a bit tonight? The RC on Saturday night is a fun place, but casual, as you can guess. This ain't DC or New York City."

"Do you only eat in one place?" asked Martin as they started to near the Seahorse Inn.

"With Frenchie in the kitchen, why would I eat somewhere else?" asked Barnett.

Williams responded, "The food has been memorable to say the least, but while on the case, we need to dress professionally. However, I guess we can lose the ties for tonight."

"That's great news," said JP as the Jeep approached the Seahorse Inn. "Could you guys just walk down and meet us at 7? It will really be worth your while. Agent Sato, can I pick you up at 6? I have something I would like your help with."

George was tempted to make a whimsical comment such as, "Ooh la la" but decided he wasn't in a position yet to be that playful with either Sato or Barnett.

Betty said, "Sure, pick up me at six," as she got out in front of the hotel with the other feds.

# 20

# Casa de Catalina Lopez

The back of the Jeep had two large boxes in the rear seats when JP returned to the Seahorse Inn at 6pm. Betty was early as normal, and had plenty of time to wonder about what JP had in mind for one hour, from now until dinner.

Barnett greeted her with, "I am glad to see you left your coat in the hotel and have that white shirt untucked."

"I need it out in order to cover my service weapon. I think I can be more casual as it's Saturday night. But I still need my badge and gun. Just regulations."

"And your phone?" JP asked her.

Betty turned her left side to him and pulled her shirt tail up to reveal that vital digital equipment in question, sticking out of her rear pocket. JP could not help but think, *How many women have a phone that's bigger than their ass?* The tiny agent sat that small derrière in the passenger's seat and JP headed the Wrangler south down A1A.

"Betty, those boxes are full of stuff that we need to put in Catalina's house before dinner. Just in case she decides she needs to go back to get something, although I do not think she will. Donna had help, and we have more stuff than I even asked for. Seems Steve and Frenchie went to Cathedral Basilica and found a synthetic ear."

"What will we do with all these items?" asked Betty.

"We will arrange it in a way that it will frighten away Satan or any of his demons," said the deputy as he grinned.

"And you know what scares the devil? "

JP turned and smiled even more. "Well, I am tempted to say it's an Asian woman with a gun and a huge phone who has access to killer bees and murder hornets. But I am hoping it's onions, garlic, peppers, statues of the virgin, crucifixes, prayer ropes, a painting of the Archangel Michael and holy water. Because that's what's we got."

Betty hung her head a bit. "I haven't heard from Dr Cohen. I really hoped I would have by now."

"You never know, there might be a good word at any time. I have talked to him. No change yet. Talked to Carol too. She's getting over the stings and, good news, there's a guy that has taken an interest in her. He comes often and sings her songs."

Two blocks south of the turn for the RC, JP swung the Jeep west down a narrow street and within half a block turned south again on a gravel road nearly wider than a car. A sign announced at once "Dead End," which could easily be seen 300 feet ahead. Six small frame houses on each side, not trashy at all, very well kept. A neighborhood the length of a football field and barely wider.

Sato commented, "This looks like nice little neighborhood, and it seems new."

"It is about three years old. There are about three acres here that were purchased by a Massachusetts Real Estate Investment Trust. They built the houses, and they also invested in building a local memorial playground with a baseball field, buying an old large southern house that they converted into a business, and they made a nice addition on the pier. They are very nice people and the tenants on this street all have leases at $99 a month until 2037."

Betty had no idea what a REIT did, or how they did it, or why. But Sato wondered why a group from Massachusetts would invest in so many things in Crescent Beach, and how were the assets JP listed a good investment? The female agent was glad she wasn't in business, as it never really made sense to her.

It should have taken no great detective, nor even junior FBI agent to spot the Lopez residence. Our Lady of Guadalupe statue in the middle of a well-kept yard, large wooden cross in the middle of the front door, and several small rock gardens with cactus instead of the palm trees typical to the beach. Upon entering the house, JP noticed nothing different, as he had visited often. Agent Sato on the other hand was a little surprised that above every doorway there was a cross with the Savior, a crown of thorns on his head. Each room was painted in bright and lively colors, many beads and other decorations abounded, and a general warmth radiated that made Betty jealously feel the love in this small house.

As the two detectives went to every entrance, where evil spirits might enter, they attached onions, garlic, and red peppers. JP splashed a little water from a typical sports bottle and picked the special places for statues of the virgin, crucifixes, prayer ropes, and the painting of the Archangel Michael.

Upon leaving Casa de Lopez, with Betty following, JP went straight to the tailgate, opened it and pointed to the yard and commanded, "Do it." The Barbets knew exactly what to do, and after a bit of circling, left two large brown presents. Sel and Poivre receive praise and two biscuits when they reentered via tailgate.

Driver and rider took their seats. The latter was curious, "Are you going to leave that in the front yard"?

JP turned to her and smiled, "I heard el diablo has a bifurcated tail. I am hoping each side is blessed with mierda de chein" then laughs at his own joke, which is just as well since Betty does not get it.

"We just have time to get Steve down for the evening, put up the pups, and get to the RC in time." Barnett threw out these thoughts as he threw the already rolling Jeep into second and put the pedal to the floor.

A bit nervous with the driving, but much more curious based on what she had just seen and heard, Betty inquired, "Can I ask? Do you believe in God?"

Normally JP would pull on his goatee for effect when answering such a question, but he was too busy driving. So, he had to settle for just saying, "I really don't know, but I do believe in heaven, and I know what it's like."

You would think agent Sato could have seen this coming, but the truth is reading people wasn't her strong suit. "Really? Can you tell me about it? I would really like to know your beliefs."

"Hmmm..." JP started for effect, then continued with what he already had planned, "In heaven it's warm and sunny most of the year, only cold long enough to remind you how lucky you are that it is normally warm. With you, in paradise, there are lots of good friends and you have a purpose and a feeling of contributing. There is lots of heavenly music and fabulous food every day. And every Saturday night there are violibobs and excellent blues plus profiteroles for dessert."

Betty said, "OK, I get it. You cannot answer a serious question."

JP did his best impression of being offended. "Oh yes I can! Did I mention that in the promised land you can hear and see the ocean every day and go surfing whenever you want?" With that he turned the Jeep into his front yard and honked a small tap at Steve who was waiting by the front door. Sel and Poivre did not wait for the rear tailgate to be open. Instead, they bounded over the rear seat and out the passenger's door openings.

Betty commented, "It looks like Steve and the dogs are ready to go in."

As the two new human arrivals walked up behind the canines, Steve said, "JP, I had a busy day. helped Catalina watch her boys. I like them, Juan is really cool. Then I helped Catalina check into the Seahorse Inn. "

Steve looked down at his feet and went on, "Then I walked back to the RC, but you were gone. And guess what?"

JP waited a good amount of time to make sure he was not stepping on the next thing Steve wanted to say, then replied, "What?"

"Frenchie gave ME an EARLY order of violibobs."

"WHAT?, You are like the luckiest guy in Florida," Barnett said as Steve stood a bit straighter and produced a self-satisfied look on his face.

"JP, that is not all. Frenchie had me ride with him to a church by the fort. We saw a a a ahhhh a priest and he gave us some holy stuff. Then we went back to the RC. And guess What?"

The deputy did not wait as long to answer, as it was clear Steve was repeating the last exchange. "What?"

"Frenchie gave ME an EXTRA order of violibobs!"

"WHAT? WHAT? You are the luckiest man in America. No, you are the luckiest man on earth!"

Steve seemed a bit concerned and opened his mouth a bit. JP and Betty waited until he spoke. "Do you think it is fair? Will it bother anyone? Does it bother you?"

"Steve, you earned those extra violibobs. Everyone knows that. Me and Frenchie know it full well. You have done so much this week, that we all must thank you."

Steve smiled and simply returned to his nightly routine, "Can you and Sel and Poivre play 'Billie Jean' while I fall asleep?"

JP responded the same as the last 100 times, "That's a great idea. We will try and see if we can," knowing they could.

Steve and JP headed down the small hallway that led towards the 'secure' bedroom.

When JP went straight to the Bongos and started the intro to "Billie Jean," Sel and Poivre ran to the corner by the saw and grabbed in their mouths two large drumsticks. Still amazed, Betty watched as the dogs ran from tube to tube, each in its own pattern, pounding out the familiar tune.

JP stopped his drumming and then with one hand made a circle in the air that his furry musician friends could see. The two law enforcement officers exited and went to the Jeep for a quick trip to the RC, where the local law expected a nice relaxing and delightful evening as usual: Saturday blues night with violibobs.

# 21

## Unwanted guest at the RC

Robert Burns wrote, "The best laid schemes o' mice an' men / Gang aft a-gley." JP had no reason that he knew of to think about that, so, he didn't. Instead, he thought about how every Saturday evening at the RC for the past year and a half had been relaxing and delicious, courtesy of Darryl and of course the famously delicious treat made only by Frenchie. This might not be a 'best laid plan of mice and man,' but rather just a typical expectation of continuity. However, as many know and all experience, the expectation of continuity is often overpowered by the second law of thermodynamics, specifically, that all things trend toward disorder.

When the Jeep pulled up in front of the RC, there was no place to park, which was no problem, JP just double parked. The Wrangler's owner was fairly certain there would be no ticket, tow, or wheel lock. The front door had potential customers walking away, those that lost their chance to get a table or a seat this Saturday. Of course, the deputy knew his table was secure. Sure enough, when Barnett and Sato walked through the door, his normal four top had two empty seats and two seats occupied by FBI agents.

Darryl was delivering the theme of the night: blues. Joan had been convinced eighteen months ago that her rock preference could be set aside on Saturday nights. Every table in the RC was taken, and some were being shared by people who did not arrive together, and no one was planning to keep track of who left with whom. The pool table had the top covered with what looked like the folding top of a ping pong table which had been painted black. Bar chairs that were just a bit too tall for the height of a pool table had been arranged around the large rectangle.

As the late arrivals walked up, George said, "About time you guys got here, you've already missed some great music."

Just as Williams opened his mouth to concur on the blues and comment that he had actually never heard better, even in the Big Easy, Joan ran up behind Betty and put her hands on her shoulders. With her head next to the agent's hair, the proprietor said, "Hey, JP. I am glad you showed up and brought this cutie with you. We are starting to serve right now." Ms. Jett made an air kiss next to Sato's ear and swiftly headed to the kitchen.

Mary was working the bar again tonight, and she had three girls delivering drinks of all type. But most got her Saturday special: "easy summer punch," which was not sweet at all like most drinks of its type, due to lots of lime juice with tangerine and cranberry powered by peach flavored vodka. Seeing her part-time boss, Joan, withdraw from the table of her full-time boss, Mary headed over with a large carafe of 'easy summer' and four glasses already filled.

As she sat down the drinks, Mary said, "Agent Williams, you strike me as the type that doesn't go for sweet drinks. Try this and if you don't love it, I will bring you wine, beer, or whiskey," and she made sure the special agent saw her wink as she delivered her message.

Betty said, "Wow, this is good. I like this!"

At that Martin knew what to add: "You should watch out. This is likely stronger than it tastes." Then, feeling he might have sounded more like a father than a colleague, Williams added, "Plus, if you drink it too much, that carafe will run out before I get my next glass," as he took a big gulp. The three others laughed, not at the lame attempt at humor, but at the buttoned-downed special agent loosening up.

Same as Mary had extra girls helping at the bar, Joan had two high school boys running the main course: to the bar, to the pool table and to the dining room. However, Ms. Jett personally brought the four plates on a tray to the law-central table, because she always served JP, and also because she wanted to flirt with Betty. As Joan set down the plates, she saw her nemesis enter the RC.

When the door opened two women moved confidently to the bar and pushed their way between two already occupied bar stools. One short, in jeans that looked to have been painted on, with a stretch skintight top and a long braided blond ponytail that hung past her round bottom. The other was very tall and built to last, with black leather pants and a black leather shirt, covered in chrome zippers, fire red super curly hair, and several heavy chrome rings on each hand.

JP jumped to his feet and held his hand up towards Joan, who was already propelling herself towards the bar. Flashing his hand open with fingers apart, Barnett yelled, "Please, go to the back and give me five minutes." The restaurant owner saw no reason she should retreat. Barnett repeated, "**PLEASE!**" Joan stomped her foot and stared at JP long enough that three of the six vodka shots in front of the two intruders where downed.

JP turned to the bar in time to see Tasha already throwing her chest into Darryl's face as the blues stopped. George said to his fellow agents, "I think that's the Iron Stripper," and he didn't really mean he thought, he knew. Even before Sato did her phone research, Gonzalez knew this was the famous ex-dancer whose blog, Facebook, Instagram, and YouTube videos of Tasha Smirnoff on her custom Harley Road King visiting 'gentlemen's clubs' across the south were legend. The clicks and income had dropped in the last few years, but it was still better than spinning on a pole in your 40s.

By the time Barnett was to the bar the big woman had planted a kiss square on the guitar player's mouth in exchange for her special request. About the time JP and Tasha hit the same spot on the bar the musical tone changed to loud and aggressive, with Darryl screaming the open lines to Dancing In The Dark.

JP, on the other hand had plenty to say. "I thought we agreed…" But before he could finish, the ex-dancer and current internet marketer replied, "Sure, we did, but you asked me to find out and I did. Diamond has no idea where she lost her lipstick. She has dozens. Plus, she has been working a corporate yacht gig off the coast of Miami since Thursday." Turning to the dining room, Tasha continued, "Are those your FBI friends? Hmmm, I did you a favor. Send the hot Latin one over, and I will leave right after."

JP was trying to agree, but the wild woman had already loudly joined in with the guitar player at her favorite part of the requested song: "You can't start a fire / sittin round crying over a broken heart / this gun's for hire, even if we're just dancing in the dark."

The deputy pointed to George and signaled for him to come over. Gonzalez gladly got up and headed to the bar. Passing midway, JP threw out, "Tasha would like to talk to you." Of course, Barnett had no idea what this clever gypsy biker, promoter and marketing magnet was thinking.

A couple of feet from the table the deputy saw an alarmed look on Williams' face, and as he swung around Tasha was leaning over the bar, hands behind her back with George's cuffs on her wrists. JP started to plant his hand in his face when Martin shot past him. The deputy tried to grab the special agent's arm and offer help. "Martin, let me end this."

Williams refused to give way, which he really should have done. The special agent charged up to George and demanded an explanation. Within thirty seconds, Tasha was uncuffed and out the door with her gal pal.

By the time the two FBI agents were back to the table, Betty was enjoying her second 'easy summer punch' while JP was finishing off his first violobob.

# 22

# Frenchie is interviewed

The perfect next choice by Darryl was the BB King classic, 'The Thrill is Gone.' It helped JP calm down and get refocused on enjoying the evening. Not even the heated discussion of the returning agents was going to spoil this man's favorite meal.

"OK, you guys, house rules. None of your petty crap before you finish this dinner, so shut up and eat."

Williams looked down at the plate before him and saw three bamboo sticks, each with five cubes of charred pork loin, a pile of traditional-looking fried potatoes, four cubes of mango with toothpicks in them, and a small cup of a yellowish sauce. "It looks nice, but I really need to cover what went on while it's fresh on my mind."

Sato had never been even close to defiant with Martin or George, so shocked would hardly convey the look on their faces when she spoke up, "I really don't think you need to cover anything now. It would be rude. We should eat, drink and be merry." Betty covered her mouth and giggled, then added, "Seriously, the facts will not change, and after eating we will have plenty of time to cover all details."

Williams stood up and headed for the bar. "Agent Sato, you better slow down on the punch!" George began to eat is first violibob and a look of amazement covered his face.

After finishing his first, Gonzalez interjected, "JP, how the hell? I mean what the shit? These things are insane. It's like they are crusty on the outside with a bit of a bite, and tender juicy inside. It's sweet and spicy at once." The Latino agent looked with envy as there were four on the deputy's plate. Everyone got three violibobs who ordered in the RC Saturday evening, except one special customer who got five.

JP picked up one of his violibobs and put it on George's plate without speaking, then continued to enjoy his own dinner with an occasional break to refill Betty's drink. To be honest, he was enjoying the apparent release of inhibition on her face, including the mouth covering and small giggle that seemed to be increasing.

Williams returned with a shot glass in his hand, four fingers deep. "Mary was right, I am more suited to whiskey than punch. But Betty, you need to start eating that pork and toning down the fruit and vodka mix. I'm just saying." On Betty's plate, only a couple mango bites were gone, and maybe a few fries. "Seriously, let's both see if these whatever bobs are as good as they are billed."

All four at the table proceed to eat with no conversation except the occasional, "Holy shit" by George. As the plates started to empty, Williams weighed in on the food, in his own way. "Deputy Barnett, I will need to interview this so-called 'Frenchie,' which I assume is an alias. It's imperative."

"Well, if you want that type of intelligence, you may need to resort to waterboarding. I have tried, and believe me, he's a hard case to break."

"I will not want to use torture, but if that's what it takes, so be it. Let's start with a material witness warrant."

JP waved Joan over. "Joan, would you please go to the kitchen and tell my brother that he needs to come out and talk to my friends?" Joan was still pissed over the Iron Strippers destruction of her normally relaxing and profitable evening. Putting her hands on her hips and dishing out the evil eye, she stomped on the floor once, turned and headed for the kitchen. JP could not help but notice how her backside looked when walking like that. Betty noticed too. Oddly the two other agents were too busy, one sipping some Crown and the other chomping on an almost bare bamboo stick.

JP started to explain what's for dessert: "It's a typical item in France, but I have never seen them served in Florida, at least like Frenchie makes it. Seems simple, but so fabulously delicious: thin flaky puff pastries full of vanilla ice cream and covered with dark chocolate crust that is crisp. It may sound simple, but they are fabulous."

"It's profiteroles," interjected Martin. "You may not see them here, but there are a few good restaurants in New Orleans that have them. Many rave about Mr B's Bistro. Myself, I love them at Mon Ami Gabi."

Mysteriously, there was suddenly a small older Asian man standing behind JP. "Frere, tu m'as appel." Turning around, the deputy responded, "Oui, ce sont mes amis," then, addressing the table, "Guys, this is Frenchie, the magician who runs the RC kitchen. Frenchie, these are FBI agents I am working with." as Barnett introduced each fed by name.

Williams looked at the Vietnamese man and discerned that he is between 40 and 65. He said, "Ca va" and got in return, "Ca va, tu parles Francais?" Martin smiled as he faced the fantastic chef, "Oui, ma grand-mere etait d'Haiti et a insiste pour que j'apprenne."

Sato said loudy, "Can we switch this conversation to Japanese?"

All four guys laugh, partly at what she said, and partly at how she said it while clearly under the influence of vodka. JP agreed with her implied comment on how rude they were being. "She has a good point, and there is no reason we should be rude. Frenchie, Special Agent Williams wanted to talk to you about your recipes. I told him they were secret, but he started to threaten massive governmental pressure to extract what he needs to know." And with that JP turned the interrogation over.

Williams looked very closely at the food sorcerer. "I do have a few questions about recipes, mainly one, but I also find you interesting already. What's your story?"

Frenchie said, "My story? I guess it's either simple or complicated, depending on your point of view. In 1975, when I was five, I was either saved or kidnapped, depending on your point of view, by Monsieur Barnett Senior. Then taken from indo-China to Florida where I got to have a normal or strange childhood, depending on your point of view. Then I had many normal or strange jobs, depending on your point of view, which concluded with me ending up here where I belong. Que sera sera. That's my point of view and my story."

Martin said, "I would love to hear the details. You seem like a very interesting and clearly talented man. Can I just ask one recipe question?"

"Oui, however, I might not answer. Is that fair?"

"Of course. Most things I have had here, I can guess the ingredients. My mother and grandmother were very good cooks, and I like to think I learned from them. The violibobs, I can taste in the marinade, cayenne pepper, white pepper, soy sauce, ginger, brown sugar, lime, but there is something else I just can't figure out."

Frenchie looked closely at Williams and tilted his head. "You have a keen palette, but there is no brown sugar. Yet two other items you missed." The chef moves his head next to the special agent's ear, then whispers.

Williams eyes sparkled and he instantly reacted. "No shit!?" There were many questions and comments and ideas that he wanted to convey to Frenchie, but before he could say anything his tipsy colleague jumped up, holding her giant phone.

Sato called out, "Wow, how cool, you guys are going to be famous!" She proceeded to lean over and hold out her phone screen. "**Look at this. So cool!**"

When Betty pushed a button and moved her hand, even at the odd angles, all of them could see a YouTube video that recounted the encounter between Tasha Smirnoff, George and later Martin. The background music and noise of the RC was crystal clear. Only 1 minute and 45 seconds, but the message was clear, and the view count was rolling fast.

Sato jerked her phone back to her face as soon as it ended, staring at the screen. "OMG, this thing is so viral. 1.5 million views and going up like lightning." Williams reached over and grabbed the phone, and won the short tug of war.

"Holy crap! **IRON STRIPPER CUFFED BY FBI IN FL BAR**!" Martin yelled as he pushed the button to replay.

Betty, the agent whose sensitivity has been numbed by easy summer punch, responded, "Yeah, clever title. That is great click bait. I bet she makes a ton off this!"

Outraged, Williams screamed, "George, you idiot! We are so screwed. And this thing makes it look like I was helping you."

Feeling the need to get right over to his boss's side, Gonzalez jumped to his feet and kicked his chair back to the table by the bottom rung. He was too young and strong, or the chair too old and weak. The round long wooden tube broke and flew right in front of Joan Jett as she approached the table to see what was going on.

That's when all Hell broke loose.

# 23

# I see Nothing

As the two pieces of chair rung flew across the floor, sliding to a halt right in front of Joan, she turned completely white, so white that in her typical black top and pants, she looked like a dark chocolate coconut cream that had been snapped in half.

JP jumped to his feet and ran up and grabbed the two pieces of wooden tubes from the ground and yelled, "LOOK, I found num chucks!"

By which he meant, these things are nothing like a broken in half baseball bat lying in the street beside a young boy and his father. (as that was what JP assumed they looked like to Joan).

Thinking quicker than the anyone else in the room, most of whom had no idea what was happening, he spun around and yelled to Darryl, "Time for kung fu fighting," and began to sing while waving the sticks in his hands: *"Everybody was Kung fu fighting."* Thankfully the guitar player picked up the message by the second line. He switched from blues to the fast-paced reggae hit from 1974. The distractor-in-chief continued, *Kung fu fighting,"* JP sang badly was the only verse he knew, and that one line had to go on repeat.

Darryl jammed on, and luckily the vibe caught the attention of two Saturday night regulars. Half-baked and on the road to plastered, Admiral Hev-Ho in his signature sea captain white hat and his first mate Miss Leopard Skin Tights decided to jump to the floor and dance. This brought on laughter and encouragement from many at the bar and in the dining room.

The volume pumped way up. Two other couples had left their barstools and started to dance. Several in the dining room were adding their voices to the singing.

Joan, George, and Martin all had mouths wide open. Not Betty Sato. She stood and started with a few kicks, then went into rapidly changing memorized forms. Most would think it was some kind of weird out of place dance, but not Williams and Gonzalez. They knew Aikido when they saw it. Each had been given the same treatment: encouraged to take a swing at Betty and then seamlessly been flipped over and thrown to the ground by a woman half their weight.

The music and crowd got louder as repeat #3 began. The singing deputy saw color returning to Joan's face. By which time Frenchie had appeared and was pulling a mushroom from his apron.

To most people a cook that had a mushroom would not be surprising. Special Agent Williams, however, knew what he was seeing, even in the limited lighting of the RC at night. The long slender stem and whitish-grey cap… should he act on his suspicion? That's when Martin's mind was flooded with thoughts of watching *Hogan's Heroes* reruns with his mother and laughing like crazy whenever Sergeant Schultz said, 'I see nothing,' which was every episode. Maybe JP was right. This special agent was not with the DEA, at least tonight.

As it became clear that Joan was clearing her thoughts, JP held the sticks behind his back as he moved to the beat, those unexpected reminders of a tragedy disappearing as they migrated to the kitchen thanks to the stealthy chef 'Frenchie,' who took them away.

"I have heard enough of this CRAP!," screamed Joan, who had turned from white to red as quickly as a Canadian on the Florida beach. Now in JP's face, "You talked me into relaxed blues night! It's not crappy dance music night! Keep this up and I am changing back to rock and roll EVERY night."

Confident he had done his job; JP held his right hand in the air then turned around and drew his left index finger across his throat. Ever mindful of the power of music, Darryl transitioned to Muddy Waters, his favorite blues artist. Once more facing the angry proprietor, JP said, "I am so sorry. It will not happen again. Could we get our desserts so it can get my friends out of here? I think the FBI gives them strict bedtimes."

Ms. Jett said, "It sounds like a good idea, as long as you don't start that dance garbage again while I'm in the kitchen." As the relaxed atmosphere returned and the reason for the last outbreak exited the dining area, JP turned to the agents and patted the air with his palms down. To which, all the agents sat down and tried to relax.

As JP took his seat he said, "Can we please just enjoy our profiteroles and relax? It would be better if we can get through the evening without any more drama. Maybe we can just talk about something else. Let's stay fun and pleasant."

Sato started to speak, and George put his hand on her arm, making room for his topic: "Martin, are you going to share what you learned about how to make those pork stick things? I really want more of those and would love to know how to make them."

"Agent Gonzalez, I still have a bone to pick with you about something much more important than food. The bureau will need a complete report on that damn video, and likely we could both be subject to an extra psyche evaluation."

JP stood up and almost screamed, "Enough! We are going to enjoy the rest of dinner. Period!" Turning to Martin, Barnett said in a low voice, "I may have a way to solve your little YouTube issue."

"That's what I'm afraid of," responses Williams.

Joan returned before the conversation can take an inappropriate path, reflecting the entire evening. A tray with four identical plates plus four small cups was set on the edge of the table. Each diner got a large white plate with three perfect pastries as promised.

"I guess business can wait," said the senior agent. "These profiteroles look authentic, and I bet they are fantastic."

Sato had a small cup in her hand when she said, "Yuk! What is this?"

All three guys said at once, "Espresso."

"Well, I hate it. Can I just get more punch?"

All three guys said at once, "No!"

Then JP added, "Just try the dessert. I will try to get you a nice hot green tea."

Betty said, "Oh great, get the Jap girl a green tea, how nice!" Then she got up and headed for the bar and once there a barmaid with a head of hair just like Bob Ross greeted her with "What'll ya have?" Before ordering, Sato looked down and saw the woman with extra hair was short two fingers, so, the tiny agent turned around and looked at JP, who was trying to figure out what could go wrong next.

When she turned around, the barmaid, who knew exactly what Barnett must have told this little chick, said, "Listen sister, you make a joke that starts with 'you OTTER do this or that' and I going to come over this bar and kick your ass."

Agent Sato was having none of it. "You attack an FBI agent, and that can land you in federal prison for five to ten years. You attack THIS FBI agent, and that can land you in the hospital for five to ten days. So, you OTTER get me a glass of punch. And if you get any of that excessive hair in my punch, that can get you five to ten trips to the barbershop."

The barmaid broke out laughing and said, "I like you, you've got spunk," as she poured a large glass of 'easy summer punch.'

Returning to the table, Betty found the conversation like the dessert: small, creamy and semi-sweet, with no rough edges on the outside, which was too bad, as she was starting to feel feisty. But after a bite or two, she started to relax. It seems profiteroles had the mysterious quality of releasing long slow thoughts such as:

*I'm having such a good time. Last time I had this much fun was with my sister. Why does she have to live in California and work on AI with Google? Maybe I should consider their offer. What is with JP? He calls the Asian guy brother and he's white. Wonder if he is interested in me, or thinks I am a bitch?*

Or thoughts like, *It's a super long drive from DC to here. The bureau has a big office in Miami. Maybe I should ask for a transfer. Mom would love that. Miami to here is only about four hours, and most Saturdays I could probably be free. Maybe even Friday by lunch. That Cuban sandwich was darn near as good as these freaking bobs - not really, but worth a trip also. And there is that Catalina Chica. Miami sounds fairly good. Wonder what my chance is?*

Or thoughts such as, *What is happening to my team? Without discipline there is no success, and being around craziness seems to breakdown discipline. Maybe it's like Professor Ericsson always said - 'the natural order of the universe is chaos, and it's our place to create order.' How will I ever explain the disorder that is shown in that video? What a freaking nightmare.*

Or thoughts such as, *Now that I am fairly sure who the asshole is, how do I lure them out? How do I get these Feds off my back, so I can handle it my way? Needs to be soon. Only about 36 hours before I completely lose control, as if this evening was not out of control enough.*

All this thinking and enjoying dessert left everyone ready to go, which JP could tell and completely supported. Standing up and pointing to Joan as she walked by, he said, "Hey, we are cutting out. Please put this on my tab," to which he got more of a response than he expected as he headed for the door followed by agents number 1, 2, and 3.

Joan Jett yelled loudly, where everyone in the RC could hear, "It is already on your tab at double with a huge tip. Plus, you covered Admiral Hev-Ho! Don't be surprised if next Saturday night it's the Velvet Underground all night! Lou Reed is almost as hot as your Asian chick."

# 24

# Takes much extra work

As the group went through the front door, Sato rushed past the others. "I call shotgun," she said as she jumped into the Jeep. Williams and Gonzalez looked at each other and shook their heads. Barnett observed, "Seems like someone feels like a kid again," and laughed a bit.

Once they were all in and the Jeep fired up, Martin advised, "Better turn around normally. You don't want to throw anyone out," which was clearly aimed at his colleague that was already leaning her head out the open doorway.

"I love the feeling of wind. It's so great." Betty turned to JP and added, "Let's drive on the beach again. That's fun."

Starting to explain while the Wrangler turned onto A1A, "Driving on the beach is only allowed in…"

Interrupting, Betty said, "Hey, why do you have stick shift? That's old fashioned. Automatic is cleaner, easier, more efficient, and that shifting takes much extra work."

JP saw the perfect opening for more playful banter. "Artificial insemination is cleaner, easier, and more efficient, takes less work. But still most people prefer the old-fashioned method."

"What?" Both the other FBI agents laughed loudly. Sato turned to the driver to see JP was trying to control his self-satisfied smile. Betty said, "Oh, I see. You are being naughty," as she covered her mouth in the typical way, but the noise is way too loud to be the standard giggle.

George couldn't resist. "Takes much extra work," and cracked up while trying to finish, then finally, "But someone has to do it."

Williams could only take so much of this, and wanted to move on to plans. "Deputy Barnett, when can we meet tomorrow morning? I would like to brainstorm with you and the team."

Yelling back, "Martin, Sunday is scared. At least Sunday morning. But I had already planned to pick you guys up at 10. We can go to the RC for an important event. You will like this. I am sure Sheriff Richardson will be there, and I think you guys will have something special to talk about."

"How long will this important event take, and can we get to work right afterwards?"

JP assured Williams, "About an hour or two, and yes sir, we can handle crime business right after." As the four-wheeler pulled into the Seahorse Inn parking lot, JP looked back. "And I should have a favor to ask each of you, for Sunday morning only."

The agents looked at one another. Finally George asked the obvious, "What favor?"

Barnett responded, "It's no big deal. I'll let you know in the morning. See you guys at 10. George, if you come down at 9:45 I may have an extra Percy cinnamon bun for you."

"Really? I'll be there," said the Cuban.

With the Jeep pulled parallel to the hotel entrance, both male agents disembarked. Sato, on the other hand, asked, "JP, are you taking the dogs on the beach?"

JP looked at the remaining passenger. "I always do."

"Can I come?" Betty attempted her most come-on face.

Feeling protective, Williams moved next to Betty and said, "Agent Sato, it would probably be best if you get some rest. Tomorrow I will need your research skills in full function."

"It's work all the time. Beach at night, not FBI business."

Seeing this was not even making sense nor headed the right way, the lead agent turned his focus to Barnett. "I am sure you know what impaired judgement means. I expect your best behavior." George joked, "No manual transmission." Both male agents walked towards the hotel door.

# 25

## Sato has a dream and a secret

As the Jeep pulled back on to A1A, Betty hung her head out in the wind and said, "See, George agrees, no need for manual transmission." Not in step with the jest, she continued, "You know, manual this and that, you know, stuff, will be going away. We can have, like you know, computers and automation take care of work. Things that people hate to do, can someday be done, you know, like by machines."

In order to head off the rambling, and avoid this obviously alcohol-fueled chatter from becoming too comical, he said, "Betty, do you drink coffee?"

"No, yuck. And you promised me hot tea. Did I ever get that? Like, I don't think so."

Pulling up to the front of his house, JP said, "I am sorry, the RC was out of tea," which was a lie. "I am going to let the dogs out, then we can walk across to the Annex and get tea really quick." Getting out and walking towards the door, he heard behind him, "Oh, I love your puppies. I looked up, like I mean I found out, they are called Salt and Pepper. That's so funny…" and the voice trailed off while JP unlocked and cracked the door open, so his canine companions could slip out.

While the Barbets relieved themselves in his yard and he walked back to the Wrangler, he heard the ongoing mumbling, something about taijtu, balance, earth, heaven. JP thought, *Why did I agree to this? Drunks aren't that fun, except on TV, and this woman acts like she has never had vodka before.* Which was closer to the truth than he might really think.

Barnett yelled, "Hey, let's go to the office now. We'll get you that hot tea and take the dogs to the beach," to which he got an upturned face with a kind of stupid grin. Then Betty jumped out of her seat and bolted for the Annex, which was directly across that famous coastal highway.

Just as Sato's foot hit the edge of A1A, a large strong hand grabbed her tiny hand and stopped her progress. The Aikido instinct almost kicked in, which would have left JP lying flat on his back. But luckily Betty had enough presence of mind to just stop and look back up, saying, "Oh, are we going to hold hands while will walk on the beach?"

Just then a minivan, rented from Enterprise by a family that thought they were headed to Jacksonville, flew by going south. Who knows? Maybe by the time they reached Daytona they might realize that the ocean would be on the right if they were going the correct direction.

The deputy had no idea who was in the minivan or where they thought they were going. But he smiled and didn't say anything as it passed. JP did have thoughts, many of which would be inappropriate to share. The dogs always stopped at the street to wait for JP to cross. Not so with children and tipsy women.

Once the coast was clear, all four traversed the road and stood before the Annex door in short order. JP entered a code and the door unlocked, then, holding it open, the three preceded him in, two cleared eyed and one fuzzy brained. "Sit," said the deputy.

Surprisingly, this single word resulted in the desired response from all three, giving time for JP to step behind Mary's desk. "I am glad I got Mary this water cooler that can dispense either cold or hot water," JP commented as if to himself as he picked up a large cup, dropped two bags in it and then pulled the red handle. "This will be ready by the time we get to the beach, so, we can go now."

Two understood 'go now' and were up and at the door in a flash. One sat and looked around, occasionally tilting her head down and peering over the rim of her glasses. JP walked up to Betty and handed her the warm cup. "Let's take the dogs on the beach. It's overcast and a bit chilly tonight, but it will still be nice, and they need to run a bit."

Sato grasped the cup with both hands and smiled as she got up. Once outside with the door locked, the quartet headed for the sand only seventy feet or so away. As Sel and Poivre stepped on the beach, they looked back, their master flicking his index finger. The canines ran towards the surf, turned north and disappeared.

Walking towards the sound of the waves crashing, Betty was lagging back a bit while she sampled her tea. "Hey, this not green tea."

JP, of course, knew that he had used two bags of black tea, since that would be the most caffeine he could get into the cup, other than coffee, which she would not drink.

"Sorry, we were out of green tea," he said, which was another little lie, as Mary always kept black tea, green tea, at least two herbal teas, and assorted coffees. Luckily, the tea was being consumed, the extra kick of caffeine included.

Both Barnett and Sato stood and looked to the east. Almost no light came from the small village behind them. The sound of the ocean was more omnipresent than its sight just now. Then two large mammals, one white, one black ran behind them headed south at close to 25 miles per hour.

"Your dogs love to run. I hope they do not get lost. It's very dark," observed the lady with the cup of tea.

"Don't worry, they know exactly where they are and how far to go, unlike almost everyone else."

"JP, it's very nice here. I wish my sister could see this place. The beach, the restaurant, the people. But she is stuck in California and always so busy."

"Really? Can you tell me about her?" inquired the deputy, as he sincerely would like to learn more about Sato.

Betty was very delighted that JP expressed an interest in her sister. She never thought that maybe this was just idle small talk. In fact, Sato had very infrequently been exposed to the idea of small talk. There had been always discussions with a purpose in her life.

"My sister is only one year younger than me, but we are like twins. We look alike so much. But she is the super brain. I was always working with dad to make things and fix things in his shop. My sister got bored with that and she took up computer design and software as a hobby. Now she works at Google. They had her doing basic AI that would help target ads based on user search and behavior."

"What is your sister's name? Sounds like she is smart and has a good career at Google."

"Her name is Suzy, but everyone calls her SS. Suzy Sato, get it? I started calling her that when I was about eight and it stuck." There was a faint sound and then a whoosh as two runners passed, heading north. "Wow, they have a lot of energy."

Betty seemed to be sobering up. JP didn't need to think this is a good time to say something positive. Why? Because he had trained himself to have that be his basic reflex (most of the time). Positive thinking is this deputy's superpower.
 "SS is very lucky to have a sister like you and to be blessed by sharing your good looks."

When there is very little light it is hard to see the color of a Japanese girl when she blushes, and even harder when she turns her face away. Betty had no idea how to deal with this comment, so she changed to the topic at hand: "SS is so smart, and Google seems to know that, because they know everything. They moved her from just figuring out how to direct ads to their special AI team at DeepMind. I am happy for her, but it means we probably will not get to work together on our own idea. Maybe it's my dream, but it's our idea, SS and me. But it might not happen. I just wish we could develop it. We have a plan for early cancer detection via cell phone. With my skills at device interfaces and SS on the AI and statistics, we might have a shot. Sure, I can code, but nothing like SS. And the math's easy for either of us, after all our mother was professor of mathematics, so, we had to do algebra by first grade and calculus by third.

But big data statistics, that is a specialty SS passes everyone at. So, anyway, I guess our dream, my dream, is not rather likely."

JP was getting lost, but one item had his attention focusing quickly: "Wait a minute! Slow down. You and your sister think you can build a phone that can detect cancer? Are you freaking kidding me?"

"Oh no, I am not kidding. And I am sure we could do it. And we don't have to build the phone. Most current phones are fine. Phones have way more computing power than most users realize. But of course, money is a problem. I figured out we need 12.3 million dollars."

JP could not believe what he was hearing, if he was even hearing it correctly. "Seriously, slow down. How is it possible? What the hell are you talking about? How can my phone do that? I am starting to think you started drinking or smoking something long before you showed up here."

Two dogs blasted by headed south. Betty watched them disappear in an instant, then stepped closer to JP and looked up.

"I build sensors that can take measurements from blood, skin, urine, feces, saliva, and odors, which I can Bluetooth to the phone, then handoff the data to an app that links though the net to a central processor where SS builds AI that does the analysis. Boom! It should be easy, relatively. And the more users we have the more data we collect, and the better it gets. The power of massive numbers of observations."

"I think you lost me on odors." JP looked down at her and asked, "Are you pulling my leg?"

Betty repeated, "Pulling leg," then looked down for an instant. Then Sato said, "I am not joking or trying to deceive you. It may seem unlikely. But I have given this a lot of thought and developed a plan. Let me tell you something interesting, since you mention odors. Did you know that some dogs can sense cancer in a person before it's been diagnosed by their doctors? That's from their keen sense of smell. Dogs have very limited mental capacity and no access to huge amounts of data." Sato smiled as she attempted to be funny. "Can you imagine trying to load a massive medical data base into the tiny brain of a dog?"

As chance would have it, Sel and Poivre, the two dogs named after the condiments that sit on almost all dining tables, had just finished their run and stopped at JP's feet. Betty had to think, *No way, they understood what I just said.*

Reaching down and petting each dog's head, JP turned and faced the surf, took a step closer to the ocean, and started to stroke his goatee while gazing up at the sky.

Betty moved closer to him and also looked up, saying, "Even with all these clouds, I guess you can still see the wicked woman constellation."

JP responded, "Some stars shine through and the overcast changes their colors. So, I see a completely different image tonight."

"Really?" asked Betty.

"Yes. I see a young girl in blue shorts, with red suspenders, a yellow sleeveless t-shirt, and she is holding something round in her hand. It seems to be a red and white ball."

"Kasumi? Misty Kasumi? Do you have some type of cartoon fetish?" exclaimed Betty.

"Maybe," was what the deputy said, but what he thought was, *Young, clever, naive, cute, idealistic. Does she know the risk involved here?*

JP turned around and headed back off the beach. "Come on, it's time to get you back to the Seahorse. Tomorrow will be a big day."

Right on his heels were two dogs and one agent, who offered up an idea: "I know it is a long way back to the hotel. I could stay at your place, if you like." She thought, *Oh my god, that sounds bad,* then Betty added quickly, "Although, I know your futon is not too long or wide." She thought, *Oh my god, that's not coming out right,* so, changing course, she said, "I can always just walk back. It's really close now that I think about it."

JP was smiling enough at this that he was glad she could not see his face. "The dogs will enjoy the ride in the Jeep. It's a nice night and they can cool down. I will drop you at the hotel."

The drive was short, but the entire way JP was mumbling almost under his breath, "This could be really risky. Many ox would be gored." Sato looked down as she repeated, "Ox gored," then casted her eyes over the rim of her glasses at the driver, who continued to mutter, "Drug companies, lawyers, clinics, doctors, powerful adversaries. Hmmm, but with the right venture capitalist, we still need probably a university with a medical center. Maybe if it's divided three ways, or maybe 40/40/20.

Money is not as hard as the headwinds. So many powerful interests would be damaged."

Finally, Betty laid her hand on JP's arm. "Since we are about to get to the hotel, can you tell me what you are talking about and who stands to incur loss from their ox being damaged?"

Turning quickly into the Seahorse Inn lot, JP ignored the question and jumped out, hurrying to the passenger side of the Jeep as he said, "I have a question for you, young lady." He leaned over, with his face close to Betty's. She thought, *So, this is when he tries to kiss me.*

But to her surprise JP reached up with both hands and gently removed her glasses and then turns around towards the light from the entrance to the hotel.

JP started his analysis out loud, "I was thinking: why would a woman be wearing glasses?
**A)** She needs them to see - I don't think that's your case."

Sato got out and moved to face the deputy, who turned her glasses over and over with particular attention to the oversized ear pieces.

**"B)** She wants to look intelligent - you do not need that, nor would you think of it.

**"C)** She thinks it makes her look cute or alluring - ditto, that's not you.

**"D)** The glasses serve some other function."

With that JP inspected the item of interest. "These little slots in the back of the right earpiece, the thickening on the rear of the left ear piece with a curious small trap door, thick lenses with no correction." Barnett handed the glasses back to their owner and asked, "Do you want to tell me about them, or should I guess?"

Betty put the custom eyewear back on and played it cool. "I am sure I don't know what you are talking about or thinking."

"Come on, don't bullshit a bullshitter, I can see through it. Somehow you talk to these glasses and they talk back to you."

Betty looked at him and reached out and took his hand. "Can I trust you?"

"Yes, I owe you that for what you tried to do for Carol," JP reassured her.

"OK, it's not talking exactly. The glasses are Bluetoothed to my phone, of course. They transmit what I say, but the screens, actually the lenses, are motion sensitive. Plus, the digital data can be formatted and shown on the inside of the lenses. Of course, I had to modify the phone and its operating system, and add programs that can be run in the background. The constant demands on the processor of course add energy consumption challenges…"

The inquisitor interrupted: "That's all I really need to know. It explains a lot." JP saw all this techno speak was going to quickly make him feel like a dummy.

"Only SS knows, so if you could not tell…"

JP gave his word. "I promise your secret is safe with me, Mata Hari."

Betty held her face closer and looked up, she then blinks her eyes four times fast, then shut her eyes for one second before saying, "Mata Hari, a Dutch exotic dancer and courtesan who was convicted of spying for Germany during World War 1. Executed in France by firing squad, Oct 15, 1917." Then Sato paused and said, "I assume you are saying I am like a spy, not that I need to be executed."

And they both laughed, as Betty had said something funny without trying. Seeing this was the perfect exit, she turned and headed to the door. "See you at 10 in the morning," they both said at once.

# 26

# FBI gets casual

George Gonzalez looked extra sharp when he arrived on the hotel ground floor at 9:45am Sunday morning, where he saw JP standing at the hotel desk talking to Alice in a louder than normal voice. The new white linen traditional Cuban shirt with two vertical bands of embroidered navy-blue designs went perfect with the dark blue jeans he always carried on trips, but never got to wear until now.

To the left as Gonzalez entered the lobby there were guests, a few tourists, a couple of reporters, a local teen, all getting coffee or juice or enjoying the waffle station.  Alice always took pride in having the breakfast area clean and organized every morning.

The arriving agent could not help but overhear, "You should plan that the FBI will be leaving tomorrow. Someone seems to think the suspect has moved to some beach town in New Jersey." Then, turning to George, JP said, "Hi, sorry, I thought Alice might need a bit of warning," as he handed Gonzalez a white box which held a fresh cinnamon bun. "Let's step outside where we can talk."

Both men moved to the door and stood near the Jeep. One talked and the other ate what was indeed the best cinnamon bun north of the Keys. Minutes later and the standard five minutes early, Williams walked out the door into the parking lot. A completely new look: not just a lack of a jacket, but also a change of shirt. A major change for Martin J. Williams, bright green polo style shirt with black collar trimmed with a line of gold, the black and gold matching two lines on the ends of each sleeve.

"Martin, welcome to Florida. You look relaxed and casual," came the greeting from JP.

"Well, I am neither. But since you seem to have done me a favor and I assumed YOU were the one who left the shirt wrapped on my room's door with a note saying 'please wear this to brunch,' I figured why not?"

George joined in. "Agent Williams, you look good." He'd never seen his boss except in one outfit. "Seriously, it looks great. I got a package with a note at my door too," then Gonzalez ran his hands through the air, up and down the length of his shirt and proclaimed, "The true Cuban."

Williams looked at Gonzalez and gave him a thumbs up, partly because he did look good, but mostly because Martin had been taught it was good management technique to give encouragement even if you don't really give a shit. Turning to JP, Martin was about to bring up that favor when Barnett started pointing a finger indicating 'look at what's that behind you.' As Williams looked over his shoulder, there was Sato walking down the single step from the hotel to the parking lot.

She wore a khaki jacket, with several pockets on the front with flaps held with metal buttons, a pocket on the side of each sleeve right below the shoulder, sleeves rolled up to mid-lower arm, a wide brown belt with a big silver bucket wrapped around the outside of the jacket whose tail hung below the top of the khaki pants with puffy legs which also had pockets on the sides. Betty was holding her head down and felt more than just a little uneasy.

George yelled, "Sato, you look like you are going on safari," which did not make Sato feel any better.

JP stepped up, as he was used to doing. "Betty, you look fabulous. Jane told me she had something perfect for you at the ITT, and I am glad I listened to her. She is normally right about fashion. You look so good; I just hope you don't distract everyone at the RC."

Williams could not be outmanaged by this guy, who had not done anything to change his appearance of local cracker in a Hawaiian shirt, cargo shorts, and oddly inappropriate cowboy boots in days. "Agent Betty Sato, I must say, you pull that outfit off to perfection. Extremely crisp and very flattering."

As it was sunny and bright, everyone could see as she turned her head up and smiled, her face the color a Japanese woman turns when she blushes. Betty was happy to receive this compliment from her boss. "Thank you, sir"

Barnett announced, "Alright, now that we are all here, let's get rolling. I cannot be late for brunch," and with that JP walked past the back of the Jeep and threw two biscuits in the rear compact while proceeding on to his seat.

Sato really wanted to ride shotgun, but did not want to press her luck. So, each took their standard places and the Wrangler pulled out without any trick pit maneuvers. It was only a short way from Seahorse Inn to the Raven Conspiracy, like everything in Crescent Beach. From her normal position behind the driver, Betty thought it was time to repay the compliment from her boss, even if she did not execute it well.

"Martin, you look great in that green shirt. I really never thought I would see you look that good." Then, thinking that sounded wrong, Sato added, "I mean, you look very nice when you dress right," then she thinks, *Oh no, that's not good either, how about this:* "Where did you get that beautiful shirt?"

Williams, of course, knows what Betty means, and said, "I got it in a package on my door with a note, probably same way you got what you're wearing. And I started to honestly not wear it, but since the note was obviously from JP, and he had somehow done me a favor, I decided I should play along."

JP turned to Williams and winked, adding to the positive vibe. "You do look good."

George asked, "Martin, can you tell us what favor?"

"Sure, since it involves you, I will need to fill you in anyway." Martin pulled his phone from his pants pocket and typed, then the special agent said, "I got an email early this morning from the director, hard to believe from the director on a Sunday morning, but here it is : '*Dear Agent Williams, I want to congratulate you on working closely with local law enforcement in St. John's County, Florida. I have been informed that your plan to squeeze information from a reluctant witness has been very useful to the sheriff's department. Please pass my thanks onto your team. Sincerely, Jack Flint, Director FBI. PS: Whatever you did must have been impressive to get Richardson, and the state attorney general to both email me on a Saturday night.*'"

George actually yelled, "Wow, that rocks."

Williams smiled and said, "Yep, I guess that ends any inquiry over the video, as we were just sanctioned by the director." Martin laughed, adding, "Now that I think about, it's probably worth wearing a loud green shirt for a week."

As the Jeep pulled into the already crowded RC parking lot, it was conveniently double parked, blocking in a car JP knew would not be leaving early.

# 27

# The Monte Cristo

At the front door of the RC a plaque hung over the normal hours of operation sign: 'SUNDAY BRUNCH 10:30 - Reservations Only.' Darryl and Steve stood behind the entrance after the door was pulled opened by JP.

The deputy said, "Six for brunch." Darryl knew there was no need to check the clipboard. What would this Sunday Funday be if JP didn't show up?

Sel and Poivre ran past the guards and headed to the pool room. Darryl leaned forward and peered past the group leader. Darryl commented on each customer that entered for Sunday brunch. He had learned the kids love that as they make their way to their special table. For this group, he made no exception.

"Check it! The MAN has gone Jamaican. Could he be Rasta? "

Williams just then thought, *I call myself a detective and didn't realize JP got me to wear a shirt with the colors of a Jamaican flag. Crap! Well, probably no one else will notice.*

Darryl continued his gig:
"The HUNK of Havana, Mr. Miami Vice - look out ladies."

George was flattered and just smiled as he fist bumped the musician.

Next announcement:
"Miss Lara Croft, lock up your tombs," then, as Betty passed, "or is it Dora the Explorer?"

Sato told herself, *I can look up Lara Croft and this Dora person later.*

Most tables already had assorted parents sitting at them. And in the pool room, lots of happy noises radiated from the large group of children sitting around the gaming table, still with the folding ping pong topping, but now covered with a giant white and red checked cloth. So many chairs sat around the kids' table that the Barbets could not get under, so they picked an empty spot at the floor.

There were only a few empty chairs in either the dining room or at the bar, but it was not 10:30 yet. The crew took their normal spot, which had been marked with a tent sign saying 'reserved.' Donna Reed had on her favorite Sunday dress, light blue with big white polka dots that matched the pure white collar and cuffs on the sleeves. "JP, I am glad your FBI friends are still with you. Is Sheriff Richardson coming with his darling grandkids? If so, we can pull up an extra chair."

JP responded, "You look lovely as ever, Donna. I talked to Andy last night, and he assured me he would come. But I expect him to be late, as always." Looking around at his table mates, he said, "But we do not want to wait, so you can have one of the girls bring our food anytime."

Donna lectured the impatient deputy, "Keep your pants on, hot shot, you know the kids get served first, and that's just starting." And sure enough, each kid in their seat was having a plate delivered with one small waffle, one crepe, a pile of home fries ala Frenchie, plus a link sausage that had been cut in three pieces. George saw Steve pass by carrying the plates and had to ask, "Is that what we are getting?" He turned to JP and said, "Looks good, but awfully sweet."

Donna responded for Barnett, "Parents get a different brunch. And so will you. Don't worry, you will love it." Then Ms. Reed turned and headed to the kitchen. Leaving room for a tall black woman to move close to where JP was sitting.

"Excuse me, JP, one of your little birds wants to say hi," the woman said, pointing to the 10-year-old girl by her side. "I hope we are not interrupting."

JP said, "You are never interrupting, Amy, and neither is your beautiful and talented daughter. Candice, are you ready for a really fun morning?"

The little girl responded quickly, "You know I am, Mr. JP," and then ran to the kids' table and grabbed an empty chair that two of her friends had saved for her.

Amy looked around the group and JP took the hint. "Sorry, Amy, these are FBI agents that are here to work with me on the recent events. Special Agent Martin Williams, Agent George Gonzalez, and Agent Betty Sato".

Stepping closer to Williams and putting her hand on his sleeve, Amy said softly, "Oh, I like this Jamaican shirt, and the sound of 'SPECIAL Agent Martin' is very sexy," as she winked at Williams and continued, "If there is anything you need to 'investigate', I will be sitting at the bar along with all the other SINGLE parents." Then Amy turned, walking away towards her selected spot. She passed Catalina strolling in with her two boys.

The bright yellow Mexican peasant dress with multi-colored embroidery caught the attention of a certain FBI agent. Although too shy to call it out himself, George was happy when JP did. "Catalina, I am happy you and the boys could make it." To which, the Latino woman whose residence had recently been saved from the work of el diablo walked to the table.

"JP, I wanted to come and thank you, but I know you are busy with your important amigos." Catalina held back her little boys, who were pulling her by each hand towards the kids' table. But she continued, "Father Joseph told me this morning at sunrise mass, that you had driven evil from my house. Thank you so much." She leaned over and kissed the deputy on the cheek. "So I was able to get these fresh clothes for me and the boys." Then, as she was dragged off by Juan and Julio, Catalina yelled back, "Gracias, gracias."

The RC was almost full in the dining room, and at the bar. It was completely full in the pool room, and as some children had finished quickly, the noise was picking up. Two little girls stood petting Sel and one very small boy was doing the same to Poivre.

Donna brought out four plates for JP and the Feds, while Steve, Darryl, Mary, and Donna's crew started the deliveries to all the parents. Each bunch included a Monte Cristo sprinkled with powdered sugar, sliced into four small triangles, a side of home fried potatoes, and a little blow of raspberry preserves. The presentation was flawless, but Sato observed, "This seems fairly heavy for brunch" as she saw the melted cheese flowing out of each quarter of the fried sandwich.

And one might think with gruyere and ham between slices of brioche, then dipped in egg batter and fried, that the Monte Cristo would be very heavy. However, due to the special skills of Frenchie, this version was delightfully light and crispy and tasty. And in his very elegant manner Gonzalez expressed exactly that review with, "Holy crap. Unbelievable."

As everyone enjoyed their brunch, the noise from the pool room grew. Only the three FBI agents were surprised when Steve pushed out a metal rack on wheels that held three large steel drums, followed by Darryl carrying an electric guitar and a small amp, with Mary and Donna trailing behind with two short bongo drums and some assorted sticks.

JP licked a bit of powdered sugar from his finger and turned to Betty. "Can I ask you to help me for the next few minutes?" Standing up and pointing to the pool room, he said, "I would need your help in there."

# 28

# Three Little Birds

Sato, of course, agreed to help and followed JP to the pool room, and as they got to the large wide entrance the deputy did something Betty had hardly ever seen him do. Taking his cell phone out of his pocket, the deputy entered the code to unlock it. He then starting typing. "Dang, I can never remember how to do this." He kept typing and swiping this way and that. "Finally, here. I've done it." Handing the phone to Betty, Barnett said, "I have disabled the password. I need you to keep my phone for me. If it gets a text, it will make a noise, but you need to watch it. And if there's a call, same thing."

"OK, that's easy. What do you want me to do?" asked Sato.

"Well, no matter what I am doing, you have to interrupt me and bring me the phone. Text or call, either way, you have to bring it to me. I wouldn't give just anyone my phone with full access, so no fair reviewing my browsing history." JP smiles. "Remember, I know your secret too."

"If I wanted to know your browser history, I would just ask SS to download it and send it to me." JP was afraid she was not kidding, which actually she was not.

"OK, keep an eye on my phone," commanded Deputy Barnett.

JP headed for the area beyond the head of the table where Darryl stood holding his guitar and his constant companions stood with sticks in their mouths, tails wagging. Sato looks back to the dinner room: Sheriff Richardson had taken Williams' seat at the table and Donna sat next to him as he shoved a fried sandwich in his round face. Betty's coworkers had migrated to the bar.

Stepping behind the steel drums, the leader of the main event, the guy all the kids called Mr. JP announced, "Happy Sunday Funday! Time for one I think you all know, and if you don't, just join in anyway."

Picking up two sticks, JP began to start a lively reggae version of a Beatles classic. Darryl backed him up. The Barbets started to hit their bongos with the sticks, not adding much to the tune nor staying in sync, but that's not why they were there. Anyone who does not know why the dogs were playing bongos, does not remember being a child.

Almost none of the kids knew there was an original version of this song. Most had no idea who the Beatles were, but ALL the kids knew their part and joined in as best they could.

*"Ob-la-di, ob-la-da"*

*The White Album* version only went on for about three minutes, unlike the RC version which went on for over four, due to about a 30-second canine bongo solo designed to get the response that naturally occured. Laughs and cheers of "Go, Sel" and "Go Poivre" rang out. The audience loved to see their favorite fur covered musicians at work.

Sato busily divided her attention between the phone in her right hand, the phone in her left hand, the music makers, and the unofficial interrogations going on at the bar. It seemed Amy was being interviewed by a certain Special Agent while a similar technique was being applied to Catalina by a Cuban agent.

As the last verse wound down, JP held his drumsticks in the air and raised his voice to try to overcome the inherent noise. The deputy held both arms straight up and yelled, "And now a hand for the real stars of this part of the show, THE FAMOUS BARBETS." As he pointed his drum sticks in their direction, Sel & Poivre sat up on their back legs with front paws against their chests. THE CROWD WENT WILD.

The dining room and bar were all abuzz and covered with smiling faces. What type of parent would not be delighted to see their child having this much fun? Only the type that would burn his extremely talented musical son with cigarettes on his hands and arms for playing guitar when he should be cleaning out the barn.

Mr. JP had to take control and move the show along as the joyful noise resides a bit.

"And now for today's main event"
Then louder: "**AND NOW FOR TODAY'S MAIN EVENT**"

As the kids calmed down some:

JP continued to yell, "Appearing today, in an exclusive engagement, the fabulous and much anticipated," doing a small drum roll, "**THREE LITTLE BIRDS.**"

To which Candice, Maria, and Nancy jumped up right in front of the steel drum set. At this time, it became clear to all the kids that these three girls had all worn light blue shirts with yellow shorts and white vans. They looked lovely, and seemed to glow as they each had a smile as wide as their face.

JP reached over and took the sticks from the mouths of the Barbets, and gave each a biscuit, signaling for them to lay down. There needed to be three centers of attention, not two. Then Barnett turned to Darryl, who started a tune that few of the kids knew, that most of the adults had heard, and that about anyone with a shirt like Williams' considered an anthem.

The drummer picked up on the stringed intro, then in perfect harmony the three girls joined in on Three Little Birds – and indeed none felt they had to worry about a thing.


Most of the kids were very quiet as the group performed a song The Wailers did about the year their parents were born.

The three girls gave a performance that would be long remembered. All their friends clapped wildly, their parents beamed, and unfortunately Sato did her one and only assignment a little slow. After the song finished, Betty ran up to JP. "I have wonderful news," she said, holding her phone up, "and you got two texts during the song."

JP turned red and grabbed his phone from her other hand, looked at the screen, and screamed, "Oh crap," then headed for the front door yelling over his shoulder "canines."

There were many attempts to engage deputy Barnett as he charged through the RC, but to no avail. He threw open the door and bounded down the steps followed by two fur covered balls of energy, who knew not where they were going, but knew with whom they belonged.

Within seconds the Jeep was started and racing away, so quickly that Poivre, following Sel, barely made it into the back seat.

Sato popped out of the front door of the RC and yelled, "JP, stop!" as the Wrangler disappeared down the street that led straight to A1A.

Betty flew off the porch with one leap, and although she still did not know why, she ran after the yellow 4-wheeler that was clearly on a mission. She could see the Jeep turn north up A1A, but had no idea where it was going or how far that could be. She just kept running anyway.

# 29

# The Game is afoot

Duckworth Edwards had opened his market in 1978, when almost no one lived in Crescent Beach. He loved the little beach hamlet as much as he hated his first name. Renting a small spot only twenty feet wide and thirty feet deep, he hung out the first of many progressively fancier signs. It was just two feet high and three feet wide, and it still hung in his office to this day as a reminder of his simple roots. The market is now 150 feet wide, but is still thirty feet deep, as that's all the lot can accommodate. All the signs from plain wood to today's individual boxed neon letters have had the same moniker: DUCKY'S FRESH MARKET.

When the running agent reached the beach highway and turned left, Betty saw the Wrangler turning left on 206. She didn't know the street name, but could tell, even from a mile away, it was the same street that had the bridge that crosses the intercoastal. Luckily, this woman could run for hours, and fast.

About the time Betty saw the yellow blur disappear, again, its driver was shifting and steering with one hand and trying to make a call on his cell phone with the other.
    "Andy, damn it, I wish you would answer. This is the second message I have left. Meet me at Ducky's ASAP."

JP thought he had this planned out and under control. He had made one big mistake: to trust that Sato would follow his instructions. She had clearly seen the two texts from Andrew Chen, and then freaking waited to tell him. *Maybe it's my fault,* the notion went through Barnett's mind, *I should have been more clear,* remembering the old saying he repeated in his head: *tell them what you're going to tell them, then tell them, then tell them what you just told them.* A great way to make sure someone is listening.

Swinging the Jeep left again, this time on to Avenue D, Barnett could clearly see Ducky's, as it was only twenty yards off Highway 206. He was happy and apprehensive and pumped when he saw two figures outside the market. One was wearing a nice women's white pant suit under a completely inappropriate long brown winter overcoat. Maybe ok for New England in March, but Florida, no way!

The other person was Jane, who had the person in the inappropriate outerwear backed up to the front of Ducky's Fresh Market and was reading them the riot act, as only Miss ITT can do.

JP jumped out of the Jeep as it screeched to a halt. Hearing the double time nonstop steam of ranting,
   *"I don't care if you're sorry that you insulted me. Screw that. What I know is how the hell you didn't notice THESE. Plus what the heck are you doing wearing that coat, don't you know it's like 65 degrees? And that romper doesn't even start to make sense with that heavy coat. Not that I wasn't happy you got it, hell I thought I would have a coat like that taking up space till next November. Even then, it might not get ....*

The deputy knew he had two difficulties at hand: the first was interrupting Jane and getting her to move away.

Grabbing Jane Beauregard hard by the arm mid-sentence, which everything is mid-sentence in this lady's case, and raising his voice to an almost scream, he said, "JANE, SHUT UP. GET YOUR ASS IN DUCKY'S. TELL EVERYONE TO STAY INSIDE AND TO NOT EAT ANYTHING."

Never before so treated, although often deserving, and intent on the last word, she said, *"Well, I never,"* as the fashion queen of the beach stormed in the market door.

JP stepped in the place vacated by the ITT lady, faced the one the Feds like to call the unsub, and stared straight, eye to eye. Then the deputy announced, "Vincent Bravo, or whatever your real name is. You are under arrest, and you have rights but I forgot what they are."

The guy in the women's clothes did his best female voice, which is damn good, as he said, "Vincent Bravo? I am sure that you have made a mistake."

JP was not going to let this go on. He had a plan and he was sticking to it. "Cut the bullshit," he said as the eyes he was facing started to dart left and right. "This is going like this: you get in the Jeep, I take you to the Annex and tie you to a chair, and we wait for you to be picked up and taken to jail in Saint Augustine." The eyes, that should be facing Barnett, kept looking left then right, not at the deputy.

Then JP said directly, "Oh I get it, looking for an escape route. Please go ahead, maybe you can outrun me. Or maybe I pull the pistol out of my boot and blow your head off."

Bravo's eyes were now suddenly focused forward, and the suspect decided it was best to not chance a run. He was found out anyway. *Maybe there is no way out. Or maybe there is.*

"OK," as Vincent raises his hands like he is in an old time western, "I'll follow you."

JP pointed to the Jeep, somewhat disappointed this asshole didn't run. Walking next to the outlaw that cost Carol her vision, there were still options swimming around, in two of the four brains on the scene. Sel and Poivre were not burdened with such a problem as options.

# 30

# Quick, what is the number for 911?

When Sato hits Highway 260 at Avenue D, she could not miss the yellow Jeep, no one could, it's a very loud yellow. Not even close to winded after a mile and a half at full speed, she dashed towards the Wrangler and the two people on its right-hand side. It was clear that JP was leaning towards the passenger seat and behind him someone in a brown coat was raising their left hand.

Betty could not see the syringe being taken out of the unneeded outerwear, nor could she see that it was being lifted and pointed at JP's neck. But she could see the black body that flew through the air with white teeth aimed at the arm holding the medical weapon.

Betty could see JP spin around, however, she didn't hear, or would never say she did, the quick command 'tuer.' Luckily one can easily forget they heard something one does not understand. Of course, there was one who did understand this command full well, one who is white and covered in fur.

Betty stopped in her tracks when she saw Sel jump and attach her jaw to the throat of the person whose arm Poivre had his teeth sunk into. The mix of growling and screams made Sato weak in her knees, in a way running never did. She pushed herself to run to the Jeep and yelled, "JP!"

Surprised by her arrival, Barnett figured he should act concerned, and started by saying "arret," in a normal tone. That was enough that both dogs released their grip, which still left the matter of the person on the ground screaming with their hands to their neck and blood streaming between their fingers.

This did not seem to concern the dogs, who turned and sat while staring at their master as if to ask, "Do we get a biscuit?" It did concern Sato a lot! She rushed towards the dog bite victim, but was grabbed by the arm and pulled back. JP looked at her and coolly said, "Quick, what is the number for 911?"

Betty did not find that funny and flipped Barnett into the Jeep, she thought to put him on his back, but held off. As she turned around, she saw the man who had been in the wig, which had now come off. He had stopped screaming and kicking, making no motion except slight twitches of his hands and feet.

JP collected himself, got back on his feet, and said, "Sorry, I should have not joked. But I knew Sel got the carotid artery. There was no chance to save this asshole."

"You should have let me try," yelled Betty.

And just as JP was trying to explain in a way that made it seem like he was sorry, which he was not, the white navigator decaled as the Saint Augustine Sheriff's Department pulled up and parked half in the lot, half in the road.

Williams hopped out of the passenger's seat; Gonzalez made an equally speedy exit from the right rear door. Andy took his time, as he figured there was plenty of horsepower here and he was not accustomed to moving quickly.

Special Agent Williams took a quick look around. The guy he recognized as the *New York Times* reporter but without a goatee was lying dead on the ground in a large pool of blood, his junior team member looking shaken and somewhat pale, JP leaning against his vehicle as if it was another day at the beach, and two dogs looking up at their master, one of which had a face that looked like a peppermint disc melting in the rain.

"Welcome to the party. Bout time you got here," JP said as if it was actually a party.

This infuriated Williams: "What happened here?" And then he looked at Betty and asked, "Are you OK?"

Agent Sato shook her head in the affirmative and the special agent continued, "Deputy Barnett, please fill me in on what happened here. Do you believe this is, uhh, was our unsub?"

JP looked at Williams and then looked at the dead guy in women's clothing laying in the parking lot then back at the special agent. "Damn straight, this prick was the bastard that was terrorizing our town and cost Carol Blink her sight."

Sato starts to speak "JP, I did need to tell you…"

Williams interrupted her, "Couldn't you have taken him in alive?" He looked at Sel, still with blood dripping from her white fur. "You trained this dog to…"

Payback's a bitch. Sheriff Richardson has stepped up to the group and now interrupted Martin. "I called the EMTs, but looks like they will just be taking this one to the coroner's office. Can you fill me in on what went down here, JP?"

Williams was fuming and wanted to interrogate Barnett, as he felt this was excessive force and had been planned, plus, lots of information must have been withheld from his team. Sato is excited to get a word in. George had mixed emotions about his duty to the bureau, torn between Williams and his natural inclination to be in JP's camp. Sheriff Richardson was a bit concerned that his grandkids were ok at the RC, and reassured by his deputy's ability to wrap this up before all heck broke loose on Monday. Sel and Poivre were wondering, *Where is the biscuit?*

JP took a deep breath, before starting to recap how it all unfolded. Then Ducky stepped out the market door and asked, "JP, can we come out? Everyone is getting ants in their pants."

In a very calm and low tone, Deputy Barnett responded, "Ducky, can you keep everyone settled down? Make sure no one eats anything. I will be in to talk to you and your customers and the employees in a minute, soon as I clear things up out here."

Ducky said, "Yes sir," and retreated into the market.

# 31

# Sel must be put down

As irritated as he was, Williams realized he was not in charge of the situation here. Richardson had the home turf and requested all the details.

JP looked around at the six sets of eyes waiting on him to do or say something. He decided to do the easier task first, and respond to those mostly willing to back him up, no matter what. Reaching into his cargo pocket and extracting a couple of treats, he completed the uncomplicated action that satisfied two out of the six standing in wait.

Then calmly, JP said, "There will be plenty of time to cover all the details, but in summary, I felt this guy, Vincent Bravo, was the so-called unsub. I decided to arrest him, he attempted to kill me and he failed."

He looked at Richardson, and got a rather short response from the Sheriff. "Good enough for me." Andy thought, *It's time to go get my grandkids.* He had full confidence JP can handle the details of the body, the market, etc. etc.

Williams found it hard to control his indignation, bordering on rage. "What? That's it?"

*JP:* "Yep, that's about it."
*Williams:* "I think you knew this guy was your target for days."
*JP:* "Do you?"
*Williams:* "Yes, and I think you had a plan to kill him."
*JP:* "I tried to arrest him, he tried to kill ME!"

*Williams:* "I see no evidence of that!"

JP just leaned over and reached under the Jeep and pulled out the syringe which had rolled there. Holding it up, he confronted Martin. "I am not sure what is in this, but I'm fairly certain it's not something you would want injected into you." Barnett tried to hand it to Williams and asked, "You want to take it and get it analyzed in the FBI lab? That would save the county some money."

Williams got more irate by the second, although he wasn't sure why. This was just not the way things are handled. "You have handled that evidence with your bare hands. It's corrupted." Falling back on years of training, Martin saw a problem that none of the others did. The situation was still unsatisfactory to the special agent, so, he spoke without fully thinking. "That dog is dangerous and will have to be put down."

Sel did not at all seem concerned, in fact, she was sitting with her tail wagging as the red liquid dried on her face.

Sato and Gonzalez were alarmed by their boss's insane statement. JP might be offended by such an assertion, but he knew it was just a crazy rant. Still, he found it a good spot to have some fun.

"In this state, we do not execute police officers that kill criminals in the line of duty!" announced deputy Barnett.

"What?" shouted Martin.

JP pulled his trump card and snapped, "Lieutenant Sel," which instantly raised the aforementioned K9 to her back legs, front paws forward. As always, a treat followed. Second in command was then called to attention. "Sergeant Poivre." same pose, similar treat.

The deputy turned to Sherriff Richardson and asked, "Would you tell Agent Williams, Andy"?

Richardson responded, "They are official and, on the payroll, I guess you could say. Vet bills, food, grooming, etc. And I did give them the OK to have those titles."

Sato covered her mouth and giggled, which would have received her boss's disapproval, had it not been for George's rather inappropriate response.

"CHECKMATE," yelled by Agent Gonzalez with an accompanying fist pump. That was enough to put Williams over the top.

"Agent Gonzalez, What's up with you? Your behavior has been over the line. There will be many questions to answer when we return to DC."

The offending Latino agent turned to JP.
    Deputy Barnett winked and said "It's your call."

George looked back at his boss, feeling more relaxed than he had in years, and responded, "I appreciate everything you have done for me, Martin. Honestly, I do. But I am not going back to DC."

"What?" commanded Special Agent Williams.

Gonzalez took no pleasure in it, but it had to be said. "I resign. It's about time for me to move on and do what I really want to do." George saw that Martin was shocked and almost speechless, so he tried to explain, "It's not you, it's not the agency, it's not DC, it's just that I hear my future calling me and it's not with the FBI." Gonzalez reached in behind his back and pulled out his service weapon and then pulled the case with badge and ID from his pants. The now ex-agent Gonzalez handed them all to Williams.

"So, this is for real? What will you do?" Martin responded.

JP answered that question by reaching in his boot and pulling out his .38 and saying, "Here, George. I do not want my assistant unarmed. Use this until we pick one out for you. Actually, you can pick out your own and Andy will OK it, I am certain."

Richardson laughed. "JP, you are so confident that you had already figured out how to spend that reward I agreed to. I love it."

A siren on A1A alerted everyone that the ambulance was very near.

Andy produced a simple thumbs up and added, "I gotta get my grandkids, you guys clean this up. Let's debrief this evening at the Columbia. We all need to hear the complete story. JP, you set it up."

Barnett responded, "Andy, would you please bring Lucy? Your lovely wife would enjoy a night out with the FBI."

"JP, that's a great idea. Thanks for the suggestion. Let's say 8." With that the county sheriff got in the county Expedition in time to make way for the county EMTs who were just arriving.

Barnett put his hand on George's shoulder, turned to the remaining FBI agents and asked, "Can you two handle things out here? We have to get the people in the market taken care of."

Both the FBI agents were still in different levels of disbelief and stupefaction, so uncharacteristically Sato took up the dead silence that lasted on a bit too long. "We will handle it. You and George take care of the market."

Anytime he's made a bad error, like selling that GTO he loved, or breaking up with that woman he thought he loved, or eating that fish taco that did not smell exactly right, or saying that ugly comment to his grandfather, George had an uneasy feeling like it was a mistake within seconds of the action, but when he walked into Ducky's fresh market, he had no regrets about the move he had just made. Gonzalez knew this was a decision that would be great for him, and the FBI would go on just fine.

George felt at home in a place he had never been in. Wooden stands from wall to wall that looked like they were forty or fifty years old, because they were. Each stand stuffed with fresh vegetables and fruit, and above those little handwritten sighs that announced prices, such as $1.49 a pound or 3 for $2. The back wall lined with freezers and refrigerators filled with the essentials of life, such as, frozen dinners, ice cream, milk and beer. On the right side a butcher's counter, with cuts of meat on display behind glass, and one display with fresh fish on ice. On the left side of the store there was a magazine stand across from racks and racks of chips and candy and such.

In the front middle sat two register stands that looked like they were forty or fifty years old, because they were. Around those stood two teenage girls, Roy the butcher, Gladys the checker, Alex the sacker and stock boy, Mr and Mrs Stabler, and Andrew Chen, all who were entertained by watching Jane Beauregard give Ducky non-stop advice on how to arrange the stock where the colors don't clash. '*I mean who puts red and orange and green that close together, no one that's who, because it hurts your eyes.*'

JP really would like to get through this without raising his voice. He didn't like the idea of yelling, that it might upset the Barbets that were, as always, by his side. However, with Ms. ITT at full throttle, there was no real choice.

"LISTEN UP, PEOPLE. I NEED EVERYONE TO BE QUIET." Of course, by everyone he meant Jane.

"Now, this is a crime screen. So, we are going to button this down now. Julie, Sara, Gladys, Roy, Alex, Wally, and Erica, you can all leave. But you cannot take anything from the market. Wally and Erica, I'll cover the stuff you've already paid for later, just save your receipt." Then JP looked at the window and saw the EMTs about to finish loading, and not wanting to deal with more 'help,' he had another plan.

"Jane, that tall good looking black FBI special agent out there needs to hear the rest of how the Beauregard family got to Florida." This last instruction brought George close enough to laughter that he had to turn around and hide his face.

Everyone except the storekeeper, the young Chinese boy, and the dogs filed out, leaving the now TWO Crescent Beach officers alone to get the final important details.

JP stepped over to Andrew Chen and said, "Andrew, you have been helpful, beyond belief. The info about the play you found was invaluable. But I thought Billy would be following Vincent Bravo."

Andrew smiled, "Thanks. Billy may still be at the Seahorse Inn waiting for Mr. Bravo to walk out. I thought I would be better at not looking obvious, so, I did it myself."

Barnett said, "That was risky. Glad it worked out. Can you tell me what Vincent Bravo did while in the store?"

The young boy responded, "Of course. I followed him in and stood at the magazine rack the entire time he was here. I held a comic book so he would not think anything about me. Adults like to think all kids love comics. Anyway, he stood a long time by the oranges, handling several and putting them back. That's when I figured he was injecting something into them and I texted you. Then he stood by the apples, same routine. Then the tomatoes, more handling and returning to the bin."

JP turned to Ducky. "Looks like the county needs to buy all your oranges, apples, and tomatoes. Please get those bagged up, so we can get them analyzed and disposed of. And since this is costing you most of the day's business, bag and weigh all the bananas, mangos, and melons too, the county can buy those too."

Ducky said, "I have some pears and strawberries that are a bit old. I was hoping they would sell today."

Laughing, JP affirmed, "The county would be happy to get those too. But you have to deliver it all to Mary tomorrow morning at the Annex."

"You got it, thanks JP," responded the grocer.

With that, Barnett turned his attention to the scene outside the window where two detectives were trying to figure out how to escape from the ongoing story of the history of the Beauregard family in northeast Florida. It was tempting to just stand inside and watch, but he needed to get several things done before dinner tonight.

"George, let's go out and save your ex-colleagues. Andrew, come with us; I want to introduce you to the FBI agents."

# 32

## Andrew Chen had an idea

As soon as the two large detectives, one small detective and two fur officers cleared the market door, JP yelled, "JANE, I hate to interrupt you, but I need your help right now."

The woman with the famous chest whipped around and responded "*But I'm not through. I am just to where granddad Ralph meet my grandmother Ida. It was close to here when the surveys were being done for highway 206. Did you know that before the bridge…*"

Understanding how involved and endless this could become, JP interrupted again, "Jane, there is important civic duty work that I need you to do now! Get in your car, go to the RC, and tell Donna, Frenchie, and Mary that we have taken care of the jerk that has been terrorizing the town. They should all be there still cleaning up after brunch."

"*But what….*

Barnett knew he could not let her start another thought, and interrupted, "Jane, focus on this: tell Mary to go to the Annex and send a message out to everyone on her contact list. The message is, *'There will be a meeting in front of the Annex tomorrow at 10am for an important announcement.'* Don't ask me anything, just you and your 'girls' get your ass over to the RC now. This is an official matter."

With that Ms Beauregard straightened

her back up, making the 'girls' even more in everyone's face, and attempted a crisp military style salute: "*Yes, sir,*" she said, and she turned and headed for her car while waving bye-bye over her head.

Williams exhaled an audible sigh of relief as he observed, "I think I see your pattern here. You encounter this woman and cope with her by assigning her to become someone else's problem."

JP smiled and did his best hick accent. "Ma mama didn't raise no dummy." Then Barnett looked at the rather young boy by his side, "Let me introduce you to the hero of today, the brains of the A1A irregulars, Andrew Chen."

Williams stepped up a bit and leaned over a lot, sticking out his hand to which a small hand greeted it. "I am happy to meet you, young man. How did you help Deputy Barnett?"

JP decided to answer that question. "This young sleuth, found on the internet that Mr Bravo, had gotten a lead part in an off-Broadway production of 'Some Like It Hot,' which never got produced." And seeing that Williams was not getting the connection, he said, "The two lead parts in the play are guys in drag."

In a somewhat unchildlike manner, Andrew said, "Mr. JP, it was actually your observation about the reporters non-changing goatee that put you and I on the trail. But I'm glad I ignored your instructions to have Billy and Ivan watch him. They are idiots and would have blown the entire operation." Then this child looked up at his co-operative as if to scold him, saying, "I just wish you had gotten here quicker, then I would not have had to slow Mr. Bravo down when he started to leave the market."

JP signaled his surprise. "Wait a minute, I haven't heard

about this. I thought Jane had slowed him down with her typical inescapable ranting."

The rather small child whose size and appearance hid his rather advanced thinking said, "Yes, she did. And I am glad Ms. Beauregard showed up when she did. But he was leaving before she came. As I had not seen you, I ran over to him holding a comic book and went into a long explanation about how I needed $3 for the comic but I only had $1.17. I figured any adult would relate to a child that counts out their saving to the last penny, as if a penny has any actual value today."

All four of the adults laughed out loud at this.
Williams asked, "What did he do?"

Andrew continued, "It is lucky I picked an odd number, because this guy was apparently math illiterate. He kept guessing how much I needed, and he was ALWAYS wrong. I played stupid; the same way most adults would think of a 10-year-old that looks 8. I kept asking him, 'Is that right?' He kept guessing again until he got close and I figured it was about over. Then I looked outside and still didn't see you," Andrew turned his gaze to the guy that showed up late before going on, "So, then I said to Mr. Bravo 'Oh no, lady, I think I forgot the sales tax.'"

By this time the grown detectives were laughing loudly and the fur assistants were running in small circles and wildly wagging their tails. Sel and Poivre did not know exactly what was going on, but they knew it was exciting. Maybe more invigorating than the takedown of a criminal they had just done fifteen minutes ago. They might have already forgotten that little performance.

Andrew continued, "The mention of sales tax threw him completely off, and he reached in his pocket and handed

me a five-dollar bill and said, 'Here, buy two comics.'
Of course, two comics would be $6.42. with tax, with $5 and
my imaginary $1.17, that would still be 25 cents short of the
needed amount for a pair of comics. But as I said, this man
was apparently weak in his mathematics background."

Williams was the first to restrain his laughter enough to
speak. "Young man, you are clearly very sharp. One day we
might find a place for you in the FBI," because of course
Martin felt that would be something a kid might want to grow
up to do, after all, he did.

Gonzalez felt he should support his newly ex-boss and give
him hope for the future without his right-hand guy. "Yes,
Andrew, you are a top-notch detective. I bet Special
Agent Williams can get you an interview."

Andrew Chen had to bite his tongue before he could say
*Why would I be interested in a government job with low pay
where my advancement would be based on my seniority
instead of my performance?* Luckily, before a discussion that
would embarrass some began, JP jumped in.

"Andrew is planning to become an energy
engineer, isn't that right Andrew?"

Williams honestly wanted to encourage this boy, so he
added, "I bet you will be able to help us find much more
energy." And Sato also felt that need to support his dreams
and threw in what interested her at the moment, "Maybe a
smart guy like you would be able to harness the power of AI
to aid in energy development."

Andrew shook his head and thought *Old people cannot see
the future* as he could not resist pointing a few things out:
"Finding energy is not the problem. It's all around us,
the sun shines, the waves move, the wind blows, algae grow.

There is plenty of energy. The issue is how to transport it and store it: that is the problem I will work on. As far as AI goes, it's already here. By the time I finish graduate school AI systems will be writing themself based on needs they will perceive we have before we know we have them. No future in that for me."

Being lectured by a 10-year-old was not fun even if you are 12 or 14, but for the two FBI agents it was hard to swallow. The more mature one let it roll off his back, the younger felt she had to counter with something.

Sato said, "Science is great. I believe in it. But you cannot neglect the many old ways where science has failed. For example, you may know that Carol Blink lost her vision after being poisoned. And her doctors could not help her. She was given an ancient Japanese treatment of bee and hornet strings. I just heard an hour ago her vision is returning. And it seems to be getting better quickly from the text I just got. So don't think we know everything yet, and discard the wisdom of the past."

JP stood with his mouth open trying to take this news in. Andrew Chen thought *There is a scientific explanation for everything. Workable treatments that are found through ages of trial and error can be analyzed and the causal relations can be established. It's been long known that some toxins can initiate an immune system response that fights off other toxins.*

Like the slow erosion of belief in the media, the Carol news finally sunk in, and Deputy Barnett rushed over to Betty and grabbed her and kissed her right on the mouth, shocking everyone. He then picked her up and started twirling her around in a circle, yelling, "You did it, you did it!"

Martin and George were awestruck. Sel and Poivre started

to twirl themselves around, but Andrew Chen remained cool and simply said: "When the mushy stuff starts it's time for the kids to leave," and with that the most rational person on the scene headed for his bike.

Coming down from the emotional high and realizing his top resource on this case was leaving, JP called out, "Thank you, Andrew, you're the best. Tell your parents I will be dropping by early next week."

The kid on the red BMX bike waved and sped away.

Williams said, "Now that the kid is gone, I have a lot of questions about everything that has gone on here. I don't even know where to start, this shit is so messed up."
    His accusatory stare shifted from Betty to JP to George and back again.

JP was not ready to address this. He had another project on his mind, and he was exhausted by the constant inquiry of the special agent. Barnett pleaded, "Martin, let me tell you what. We all return to our corners and relax. Get ready for tonight, and at dinner all shall be revealed. I really only want to go through this once." He looked around and everyone seemed to be in agreement.
    "OK, let's get in the Jeep and I'll take you guys to the Seahorse. We can all relax a bit and I will come back and pick you up at 7 or so."


Martin said, "George, why don't you sit in the front? FBI in the back on this ride. Not sure I should trust JP and Betty in the front together." Williams sometimes thought he was funny, when he wasn't. About like everyone.

After letting the Barbets into the rear of the Wrangler, JP walked past Betty, already seated behind the driver's side

and stopped, leaned in and said where all could hear,
"I cannot believe you pulled this off. What you have done
for Carol will not go unrewarded."

Everyone in earshot, except the dogs, wondered what the
so-called reward might be.

# 33

## Sato saw the Future

The oldest restaurant in the oldest city in America is the Columbia. The center of the old town has hosted the home of legendary Spanish cuisine since 1905. Over 100 years ain't bad for a family eatery, and still being popular with tourists and locals alike is even better. Normally it's not that easy to get a nice six top table by the inside fountain at 8pm, even in off-season. But if it's for the St. John's County Sheriff, moving a family of tourists to the upstairs can be arranged.

There was no parking for two blocks from the Columbia, and the parking two blocks away was full. So were the parking spots three blocks away. As luck would have it, JP knew that would certainly be the case. Calling ahead is not only a good idea for dinner, but also parking. No one can drive down St George Street upon which 'the gem of a Spanish restaurants' lies, but you can go one way down Hypolita Street, which passes by the side.

When the yellow Wrangler stopped at St. George and Hypolita, a short medium build woman with short brown hair ran up to the driver and kissed him on the check. "JP, it's great to see you. Get out, enjoy dinner, and text me a few minutes before you want this bumblebee back." The detectives all got out and the woman jumped in the Jeep and it was moving before the honking to the east had hardly started.

A few steps before reaching the restaurant door, agent Williams put his hand Barnett's shoulder. "JP, before we go in I want to clear one thing up?"
"Sure, what is it?"

Martin continues, "Before you picked us up this morning, Agent Sato was telling me about the neighborhood Catalina lives in. That it was built by a Massachusetts real estate investment trust that also bought a local large old house, built a playground and ball field and did work on the local pier".

JP gave Williams an curiously intense look as he felt there was more coming; and sure enough Martin continued.

"Several items started to fit together; Boston hit and run driver, dead boy and his father, wild reaction to a broken chair rung, Frenchie carries psychedelic mushroom in his apron. So my question is as I ask you before; what's the deal with the woman that is Donna Reed AND Joan Jett. What's her name and her story"

JP starts to pull on his goatee and consider his options; clearly Martin can find the details out any way. "Karen Savino"

Sato repeats softly 'Karen Savino' as she looks down and starts to blink. Then quickly turns away.

Agent Willaims looks directly at Deputy Barnett and takes a step closer as he inquires, "And you think it's up to you and Frenchie to give her illegal psilocybin?'

JP feels he has to make the situation justifiable; "Martin, Karen was just sitting by her front door every day, looking at the street where she personally saw her family disappear, in a zombie state from the legal meds that were required to keep functioning at all. Now she has a purpose, friends, and two new names. You tell me what is the greater good"

Williams was conflicted as he turned to Sato; "Betty, are you alright? "

With her back turned, her glasses in her left hand and her right hand rubbing her face; "Yes sir, I just have something in my eyes" Which is was true, the type of thing one might get in their eyes after reading a sad news story and two related obituaries.

The organizer of the evening said, "Come on guys, let's get to the table and get situated before Andy and Lucy get here." JP moved to the heavy wooden front door, which he held open for his guests.

At the hostess stand, the receptionist spotted Barnett and the others before they reached her, so she called out, "JP, the Richardsons are already at the table. You can go right in."

"Isabella, you are kidding me. We're ten minutes early and Andy's already here?"

"Yep, if it was just Andy, you'd be right, but Lucy is never late for a margarita. Have a great dinner."

Andy Richardson stood up as he saw the group approach. JP for one was a little shocked. He had seldom seen the sheriff so well dressed, in black dress slacks, a pinstriped Oxford shirt and a navy-blue sport coat. JP for the first time in years felt a little awkward over clothes, as he had encouraged everyone traveling with him to remain casual.

"Andy, if I had known it was a formal dinner, I would have at least put on long pants." Looking over at Mrs. Richardson, a fit and attractive woman that no one would peg as a grandma, JP added, "Lucy, you look lovely as ever. I guess we have you to thank for getting Andy here on time." Followed by introducing Martin, George, and Betty to the sheriff's wife.

Lucy Richardson stayed seated and said, "JP, I thought this would be a great evening to get Andy dressed up a bit and be on time. Everybody, please sit down, relax. Order a drink. I highly recommend this 1905 Rita."

As the waitress rounded the table, laying down menus, Lucy continued, "Oh, and just in time, flip this over and you will see the drinks on the other side." The waitress excused herself with, "I will be right back for your drink orders."

Mrs. Richardson said, "JP, Andy already told how you, let me say, persuaded him into getting you a relief assistant for your busy schedule," winking to let Barnett know she realized he mainly just walked around talking to people or sat at his desk reading or hung out at the Raven Conspiracy. "But this fine-looking young man cannot be just called JP's helper. Honey, can you think of a good title for Mr. Gonzalez?"

The sheriff looked up from the menu. "It's up to JP. My deal with him includes a free title. As long as it's not sheriff or mayor."

George's new boss offered his idea, "Honestly lately I have been thinking SS is a great nickname. So Super Sargent sounds good to me. Super Sargent George

Gonzalez - SS for informal situations and SSGG for those serious matters we hope we never have."

Ex-agent GG smiled and made his feelings verbal, "I love it, works for me."

Everyone looked at Andy, who understood he was expected to weigh in. "Super Sargent it is. Now George, I mean SS, get all your info etc etc to Mary. JP, you fight out the proper pay with the county comptroller."

Betty is happy she took a seat next to JP, and leaned over and whispered in his ear, "You stole my sister's nickname." The deputy responded, "She won't mind," which everyone at the table could hear.

The waitress arrived and promptly asked, "Can I take your drink orders?" And put her hand on George's shoulder.

George said, "I'll try the margarita garrison."
*Lucy:* "I'll take another 1905."
*Andy:* held up his shot glass and just shook it
*Martin:* "The old fashioned."
*JP:* "I will have what Lucy's having, the 1905."
*Betty:* "Can I get a hot tea? Green tea if you have it."

As the waitress withdrew, Lucy looked across to Sato, "Don't want to go for something a bit stronger, or saving it for the wine?"

"I recently found out my limit on alcohol is rather low." Sato wanted to seem part of the crowd, so she added, "I'll wait for the wine with dinner."

Lucy responded, "Honey, I can respect knowing one's limits. Mine is four," then puts her hand on her husband's arm, "maybe five." Looking across the table, Mrs. Richardson added, "Now, JP, I for one am ready to hear how you nabbed this criminal and brought him to justice. The hubby tells me it was very dramatic and exciting."

JP was not really that comfortable with organizing his thoughts to tell this as a professional sounding account. But he did want the Richardsons to be impressed, especially Lucy. Barnett fumbled around, "Well, it's hard to know where to begin. Of course, the difficulty to start is coming up with a list of suspects."

Andy jumped in. "Lucy, did you know the FBI thought it was JJ Cormack to start with?"

"You're kidding, right?" responded his wife.

JP did not like the direction of this already. "Lucy, to be fair, the FBI had been given false tips. I suspect that information came from the terrorist himself." Barnett thought calling the asshole a terrorist would sound more professional and make his work more impressive. "And I would like to say, much to Martin's credit, he ruled out JJ within a few minutes of meeting her."

The waitress showed up with a tray of drinks and put a new 1905 margarita in front of Lucy, who instantly took a drink and observed, "I bet he ruled her out quickly, as no one was dead!"

Everyone took a look at Mrs. Sheriff, who added, "I'm just saying if THAT woman wanted someone dead, I sure wouldn't want it to be me," and of course that called for another sip from the 1905.

A young guy showed up at the table holding a cup in one hand and hot iron pot in the other. Martin pointed to

Betty, and sure enough the hot tea was placed in front of her.

Andy said, "JP, please go on, I am sorry I interrupted." His wife added, "Oh yes, please do. Andy already did his part giving you your head in this awful situation."

JP knew it's always good to spread the credit around and so he does, "I had a lot of help in narrowing down the focus. And to be honest the terrorist gave me one of the best ideas in what to look for, without actually meaning to."

Williams was dying to ask questions, direct the course of this 'report' as he could see it was about to be as unorganized as Barnett's procedures overall. However, he had promised himself to treat this as a local matter with only tangential interest to the Bureau. So, he sat mute as the deputy continued.

"This guy stole or picked up a lipstick at a club in Daytona, then left it at the scene of the shooting as a false clue. I thought it might be a lure to start with because there were prints on the sides and the top and bottom were clean. Anyway, I had Mary drive it into the lab to check the prints. Unfortunately, it took of over 24 hours to get anything back."

"Who in the lab did Mary give that to? That's way..." Feeling a squeeze on his arm Andy turned as Lucy said, "Let JP finish. There will be plenty of time to talk to the lab."

JP pushed forward. "Well, let me see, it actually turned out really better. By the time the lab got back with the results, Friday morning, I had already talked to five people who had seen the asshole, I mean suspect. So, I knew the lipstick was a plant."

Williams jumped in without thinking, "How?"

JP continued, "The lipstick belonged to a girl named Diamond Mounds, and she's black. And that's how I got my first big clue without ever knowing it. When Mary gave me the report Saturday morning, we talked about how it could not be Diamond that Carol had described. I said there would be no way that the woman that Carol and the Gordon boys saw could actually be a black stripper, no matter how much makeup. "

Looking up and seeing everyone was paying close attention, Barnett was more enthusiastic about relaying the story. "Mary joked with me and said 'Yea, you would have a better chance of passing yourself off as a white woman than Diamond would. In fact, I think it would be fun to see you try. I have a dress I can lend you.'
    "Of course, we had a good laugh about that. What's not funny about the thought of me dressed in drag?"

This time Mrs. Richardson decided to jump in, "So, that's when you got the idea that it could really be a guy?"

"No, in fact, I just thought Mary and I were joking around." The speaker pulled on his goatee as he seemed to think a moment. "Actually, during the meeting with Andy and the FBI, I got a text from Andrew Chen, telling me the other A1A irregulars were not being serious enough. Which made me think of Andrew's father, Charles. I had meet him three times and always noticed how interesting his Fu Manchu moustache is."

Everyone at the table had a curious look on their face, and more than one was thinking *What the heck is JP talking about?* But with no one interrupting, the seemingly random thoughts continued.

"And as Andy is eating a cinnamon bun, I start thinking, sometimes I see a soul patch on the Sheriff and that's fairly cool, but not today. And I keep thinking about that Fu Manchu on Charles, it's really distinctive although always a bit different. Then we finish the meeting and get in the Jeep and head to the RC for that fabulous lunch."

George had to jump in, "Great lunch, but nothing compared to dinner. Those violibobs rock!"

JP continued, "They do! Anyway, for some reason, when I backed up the Wrangler, I caught a glimpse of myself in the mirror and thought 'time to trim the goatee.' I guess I had facial hair on my mind. All four of us walk into the RC. There at the table were the reporters. We didn't talk about them, but I looked at them."

Williams started nodding his head, as he saw where this was going.

"So, I look at Vincent Bravo twice and have to notice, 'His goatee is freakin perfect, and I think back, it's always freakin perfect.' It hits me that one way to keep your facial hair perfect is it's fake."

Williams had to get into this. "So, why didn't you let us know? Or bring him in for questioning then? Why wait?"

"I didn't really have any proof and it was just a hunch. But once I got more information it started to make total sense. So, during lunch I texted Andrew Chen because I knew he was into the internet big time. I ask him to pull up everything he could find about Vincent Bravo. By the time we all got to Daytona, Andrew texted me back a list of links to stuff about the guy. The one where he was boasting about being picked for a lead in 'Some Like it Hot' just jumped out. Of course, as the play's about two jazz musicians that dress in drag to get a gig, it all fell together."

Lucy had to comment on this. "I love the movie *Some Like It Hot.* Marilyn Monroe was so funny. The two guys that dressed as women were funny too. I just loved Marilyn."

Not interested in plays and movies, as they relate to this case, Williams jumped in again,
   "Why wait? You should have told us, and we could bring him in. That put your town at risk."

JP was getting a little sick of this, but didn't want to spoil dinner. First, it's never a good thing to ruin a meal before you even get to eat it. Second, he had more important fish to fry later. "Well, that's a good question Martin. We were already in Daytona. I had some guy at a gentleman's club to deal with, you had me on a mission about explosives, and I knew how to protect my town. I sent a text to Billy and Ivan, told them to keep an eye on Mr. Bravo. And to interfere if they saw him doing anything awful, plus, to contact me."

Williams was not down with this approach at all and made that clear. "You turned this over to a bunch of kids? The same ones we saw playing hooky to get stoned?"

Still trying to remain cool, JP took a breath and a sip from his 1905 Rita: "Andrew never gets baked, and the other boys are a bit rough around the edges, but good at heart. AND IT ALL WORKED OUT."

Lucy said, "JP, how did you know you'd catch him?"

"Lucy, the truth is, I wasn't certain I would catch him in the act. But I did know that 'an egg suckin dog, is gonna suck eggs' and I put out the word that the FBI had moved their focus to somewhere in New Jersey. So, I thought he would tip his hand. However, I was going to bring him in and try to get him to confess Sunday afternoon. He saved me the trouble by trying to poison food at Ducky's Fresh Market. And he saved the state a lot of time and money by trying to kill me."

As if on cue, the waitress appeared and put her hand on George's shoulder again. "Are we ready to order dinner?"

George was certainly ready as he heard. "Let's start with you, big boy."

*Gonzalez:* "La completa Cubana."
*Lucy:* "Chicken Salteao."
*Andy:* "New York strip, medium — oh and let's get two bottles of Don Cesar Crianza. That's a red I know everyone will like."
*Martin:* "Palomilla."
*JP:* "Roast pork 'a la Cubana."
*Betty:* "Grilled red snapper, with no butter."

The waitress stared at the last to order and said, "The lightest thing on the menu. No wonder you stay so thin," then looking up and smiling at the guy she knew controlled the town and more importantly her tip, "I'll be right back with the wine, Sheriff."

Andy took this break to ask something he had thought about. "JP, do you think this Bravo guy was gay?"

Barnett instantly responded, "Does not matter to me, but probably not, as some of the posts Andrew Chen sent me had stuff about his assorted girlfriends."

Having not really been part of the conversation, Betty decided she should contribute. "Most cross dressers are heterosexual and driven by other motivations."

Lucy asked, "JP, what do you think Bravo's motive was?"

The deputy stoked his goatee a bit before his response. "I have learned from my dogs to not think too much about why people do things and just focus on what people do. But if I had to guess, I would say it's one of three things, because most lists have 3 things.
    "1} Bravo was just crazy.
    "2} He was just mean, like maybe Linda Hood, the classmate of Mary's that stomped on a frog.
    "Or
    "3} He knew that as long as notable events were going on in Crescent Beach, that the New York Times would pay him to be on a vacation and eat at the RC every day."

JP continued, "Like I said, I am with my dogs, just judge people on what they do. Nothing else matters. So, likely it could be all three motives, I just don't care."

To which George said a bit too loud, "I'll drink to that!"

Everyone lifted their glass and laughed, except Sato, who reacted a bit slow while thinking, Why are we drinking after that statement? Does it make us thirsty? Betty finally picked up a glass of water and smiled.

After the slight diversion, JP shifted from storyteller to salesman as he felt it was time to make the move on Richardson, not Andy, but Lucy. Mrs. Richardson happened to be the daughter of Thomas Knight, the president of The University of Florida in Gainesville, which is home to Shands Hospital, whose president by chance happened to be Dr. Robert Leland, father-in-law of Lucy's daughter. Barnett had been at the wedding of Jennifer and Robert Jr in October, a huge affair. JP remembered it for mainly how he kept wondering *How long before I can leave and take off this rent-a-tux off?*

"Anyway, that's about the whole story. And I am glad it's over, because I have a MUCH more important project to work on," JP teased. "Finishing the case frees up next week, I hope."

Everyone wondered the same thing, but Lucy was the most intensely pulled in as she was being directly stared at. Mrs. Richardson asked, "JP, what could be more important? Do tell."

JP got the in he was counting on. "Lucy, I am glad you ask. I am working with a team that is designing a medical device that can save tens of thousands lives a year. Maybe even more. Just a few cogs needed to make this wheel turn. Basically, three components: the tech team, the money, and the facilities."

Andy was afraid to ask but did anyway. "How much money do you need?"

"Fifteen million," came the quick reply from the deputy.

Sato, who had barely spoken, revealed her shock. "FIFTEEN MILLION?"

JP knew he needed to steer this discussion where he wanted it. "Oh, but the money is not a problem. I have lined up a Swiss venture capital group for $9 million and another one in Luxembourg for $6 million. Now what I need is a place that has enormous computer power, fabulous medical research capacity, and access to lots of brilliant minds." Which was a type of lie, as Barnett already felt the brilliant minds were on board, as it was their idea.

Lucy put down her margarita and sat straight up in her chair. She knew exactly what JP was getting at, but must clear things up: "UNF cannot be associated with black money. Switzerland and Luxembourg smell funny to me. Not to say anything accusatory about your dad, mind you. But I want to make that clear even before we hear how this can save that many lives."

JP was right where he wanted to be. "No dirty money, I promise you that, everything above board. Lucy, this is about saving lives, not about money. Although it makes sense that there should be a return. I am shooting for 40% for the team, 40% for the venture capital groups, and 20% for the institution."

As expected, Lucy was excited and reeled in by the idea of being a part, even if a small part of a project that sounded so important. Without even knowing the details, Mrs Richardson started to bargain, "I really think that 1/3 each sounds more equitable. What medical expert have you got in on this?"

The plotter-in-chief had already expected and adjusted for the question of division of spoils, if any. However, he was completely thrown off by the second issue. "Well, ummm, I promised to not bring the team principals in until later in the process. But if you do not discuss it with anyone until the first formal meeting is set up, I could mention one, maybe."

All at the table became intensely interested, not the least of which was Betty, who had wisely decided to not get involved in something she did not yet understand. Lucy reached to her mouth and closed an invisible zipper, then pointed to Andy as if to assure his silence.

JP jumped at getting a lifeline: "Well, not to be discussed until later. But I can tell you Dr. Cohen will be involved," figuring that after tonight he might be able to get Isaac's help and support considering the killer bee and murder hornet miracle.

Lucy was very much reassured and getting even more animated as she asked, "Our Dr Cohen? Isaac is my personal doctor. Is that who you mean?" Of course, the county sheriff's wife had the head of the only hospital in the county as her personal physician.

JP nods.

Lucy was already all in on doing her part. "I will do my best to setup a meeting with Bob, Dad, your team, and the money guys. If UNF and Shands can be part of a project that saves that many people, it would be wonderful. I look forward to hearing all the details and will push my father to let me sit in."

"I will be representing the venture capitalists," JP said as he smiled at Lucy. "Thanks for taking an interest in this project. If it saves lives as I feel certain it can, you will be part of something really fantastic."

Williams had to ask, "JP, can you give us an idea of what this device is and how it could save so many lives?" The Special Agent was truly interested in this.

Barnett did his pet the goatee routine and then said, "I really want to keep this private until Lucy and I meet with my Tech Team and the UF/Shands folks. But I guess everyone here knows how to not spill the beans." Everyone nodded in reassurance except Sato, who was trying to figure out exactly what's happening and what it has to do with beans.

JP looks at Sato, then he reaches in his cargo shorts and pulls out his phone, which he lays on the table. "Imagine this thing that about everyone has in their pocket could tell if you had very early signs of cancer. Imagine it could alert you, and imagine you could go to your doctor for more analysis and early treatment."

Lucy said at once, "**I do not have to imagine what that would mean!** I will get a meeting with Bob and my father right way. This better not be some wild bullshit idea. I hope to hell you are serious."

At this point Williams saw what was going on, but he didn't dare speak. All he could do was think, *This has got to be Sato. That's the only way it makes sense. First, George, then Betty. What's with this place? Everyone seems happy here, that's for sure, kind of like I was in NOLA. I wonder what my mother, and my brother, and my old friends are doing there? The Big Easy, now that's a place that's fun and has a lot of soul, something no one ever said about DC.*

Andy felt this sounded exciting, although it was a bit out of his league. So, the Sherriff was feeling a bit left out. He was the big dog at this table, and JP and his wife were carrying on their own business, which did not seem to involve him at all. Deciding to get back to things that concerned him, he said, "JP, you have had a had a very busy week. Doesn't seem like the relaxing life on the beach you had planned when I hired you."

Thinking back three years ago when he was offered a fun relaxing way to be a part of a laid-back little beachfront hamlet, before the RC, before the Barbets, before many things that were now so important to him, JP smiled and said, "Yep, Andy, you never told me there would weeks like this. At least Monday was beautiful and normal, then on Tuesday all hell broke loose."

Andy saw another place for him to step in. "JP, everyone knows all about what happened after the shooting on Wednesday. Fill them all in on Tuesday."

This is where JP got to do his signature petting the goatee before he spoke. "Well, by Tuesday night, I thought Tuesday would be the wildest day of the month or maybe the year. It was really nice outside, so I walked down to the pier and there Gidget was setting up her business." Barnett looked at George and added, "She has an ice cream stand, which has no permits, but we let that slide." George smiled and winked. JP continued, "So Gidget and I start talking about assorted stuff. Her daughter Songbird goes by headed to the beach…"

Lucy interrupted, asking, "Songbird Wilson, the famous freestyle surfer?"

"Yes, her mother and I are good friends. Anyway, Gidget I remember is saying the funniest thing to me, something like she thinks it's going to be a wonderful year because the beginning of the year is the same as the end. Then she said, 'It's 2020, get it? Just think, the last time it was like this it was 1919, then I guess 1818, then 1717, it's just crazy, don't you think?' And, of course, I am thinking it's great that Gidget is so lighthearted."

What Lucy thought was, *I wish once in my life I could have been like that.* And what Betty thought was, *Thank Buddha that I have never been like that.*

After taking a little drink of the 1905, JP continued, "And I remember we were talking about how Songbird would certainly do great at the ValCom surf contest in Miami and win a trip to Hawaii this summer. Just chit chat like that, next thing I know a bunch of people are running from the beach yelling 'shark.'"

Williams asked, "Are there many shark attacks here?"

JP responded, "No, there are hardly any" and then continued, "So I headed for the beach and frankly Gidget is ahead of me as she is freakin flying. When I get on the sand, I see a bunch of people gathered in one spot and I run that way. When I get through the crowd, I see several people pulling Songbird on her board into shore and there is blood dripping down her arm. I look to the right and a little way out in the ocean, Steve is pulling in a tiger shark with its head cut to ribbons, it looks like a bloody jigsaw puzzle except with Steve's knife stuck in the middle of its head."

Andy jumped in, "This is the knife he took off a guy in Afghanistan, that made the fatal mistake of trying to slit Steve's throat? What is that kinda knife called again?"

JP remembered all too well: "It's a jambiya, and Steve carries it with him everywhere. Damn good thing too, as he was very determined to defend Songbird, so I'm glad he had it. Anyway, Steve had a few bites as did

Songbird, but they are both on the mend. So next month, my bet is she wins at ValCom and gets to go to Hawaii, and when she does, I am going to get Gidget a ticket. I want Songbird's mother to see how she does at the big international event."

Betty looked up from her phone and in what seemed like a completely off the wall remark said, "Well, I hope the surf contest, or flights to Hawaii, or other nice stuff like this wonderful dinner are not affected or even cancelled by the virus that's starting to be in the news. The outbreak on the cruise ship in Japan and in the Seattle assisted living facilities are concerning."

JP instantly thought, *What the hell is Betty talking about? Maybe she's not as smart as I thought, or maybe she is really a bit insane. What am I getting myself into? Is Betty going to make me look like an idiot at our meeting with Lucy and her father? CRAP. What type of person thinks a virus is going to end sports, or travel, or for god's sake eating out?*

Printed in Great Britain
by Amazon

76037002R00149